TRIBAL ANTHOLOGY

ERIC BELL

Copyright © 2016 Eric Bell
All rights reserved
First Edition

PAGE PUBLISHING, INC.
New York, NY

First originally published by Page Publishing, Inc. 2016

ISBN 978-1-68348-350-2 (Paperback)
ISBN 978-1-68348-351-9 (Digital)

Printed in the United States of America

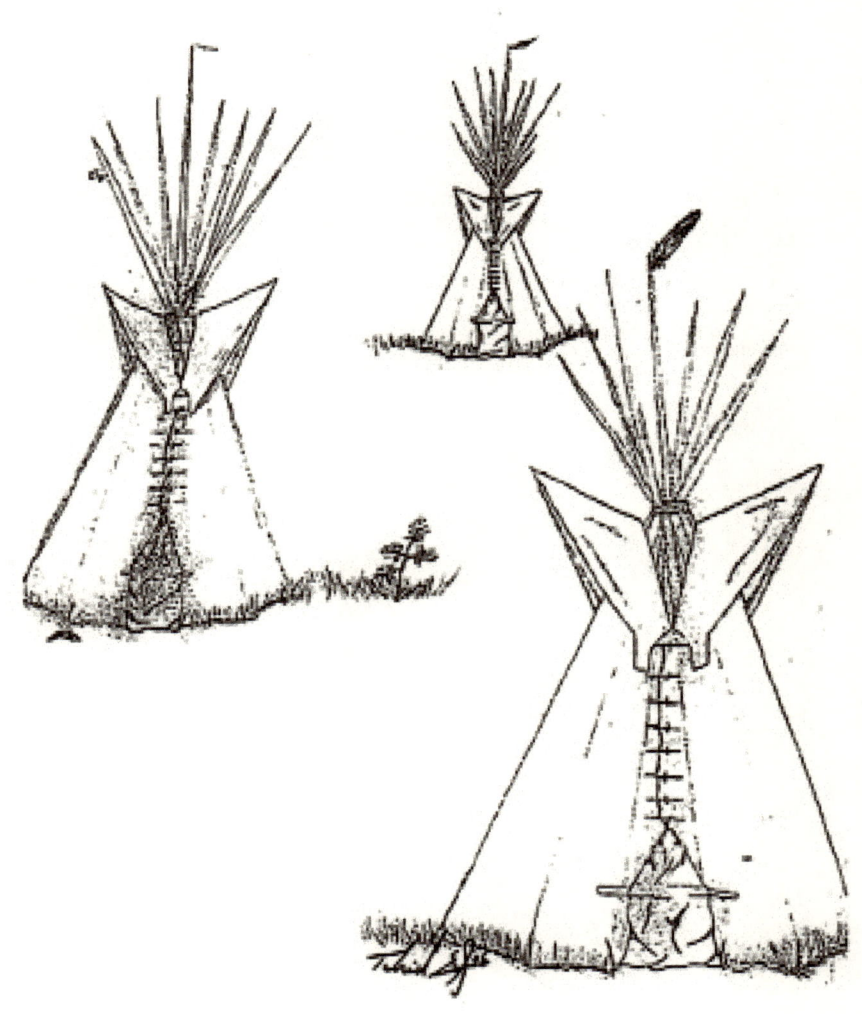

Acknowledgements

Gina Langly Phd.
Thank you for your support and your belief
in me for writing this book.

Juanita (Jaye) Arellano
Thank you for your encouragement and advice for my story.

The whole Bell family
For all they've given me to make this book possible.

Chapter One

Tribal Anthology

In a time when life was peaceful and people lived in teepees, Apache people would have fun in the evenings. After eating, the people would sit around in the teepee and tell stories, stories of long ago, when the elders were kids, stories of fun and adventure, and stories of ghosts and legends.

One story the people remembered was told by the chief elder, Running Horse. His story goes this way:

"I remember long ago when I was a teenager. I was on my way home from hunting—I was bringing home a doe, carrying it on my shoulders. When I came to a river crossing, I stopped to get a drink. When I heard a crashing in the woods, I dropped the deer and hid in a nearby bush to see what it might be. Its footsteps came closer and closer. My curiosity grew with my anticipation.

"There it stood by the river: something big and tall. At first, I thought it was our creator, but it had hair all over. It stopped to drink water, and it sniffed around, and it found my deer. It picked up the deer. Then it let out a loud, scary howl. I was too scared to move. It howled again. I had never heard anything like it before. And in a blink of an eye, it was gone. It left behind oversized footprints on the ground. I believe I saw Big Foot, the legendary giant." Everyone looked at each other with amazement and fear. Running Horse continued, "I ran all the way home in fear. I didn't look back once. That day, I was supposed to be hunting for food. I lied to my father when he asked if I had seen any deer. 'No,' I said, 'I saw no deer,' because I thought he would not believe me if I told him about Big Foot. This is the first time I have told this story."

The children showed fear on their faces but said nothing. Some of the adults showed an interest and said they liked the story and asked if Running Horse had seen the creature again. He said no.

In the midst of everyone talking about what they had just heard, a woman, middle aged, interrupted by saying, "Did you know, I had an encounter, too?" Her name was Autumn. Her best friend was named Heaven. "My story is true."

"It happened when I was little, about seven or eight years old, when the tribe was much smaller. I had a best friend. We did everything together, even went places together. We always played in the meadow not far from our campsite. One day, we wandered off from the meadow, deep into the woods that surrounded the meadow and up into the mountains, away from the campsite. We played in the woods with excitement. We felt wild and free. We were having so much fun we lost track of daylight. Soon it was dusk. We watched the sun set behind the mountain. Then we started for home. We knew home was near the meadow, and the meadow was at the bottom of the mountain we were descending."

"It's a good thing you two didn't get lost," Faith said.

"Just as me and my best friend were almost out of the woods, we ran into a little man. The top of his head came just below my waist. I suddenly stopped to look at him. He said, 'Hi.' In wonderment, I asked, 'Who are you? Where do you come from?' The little being replied, 'I come from a small village not far from here.' Come, I will show you.' I was afraid, and I said, 'No, my friend and I need to get home.' It was almost dark. Then he got mad and called the rest of his people. They were small like him. With anger showing on his face, he said, 'You and your friend are not going anywhere but to my village.' They grabbed us, and we started to fight off the little people. We finally got away. I started to run, and I kept running, thinking my friend was behind me. I ran all the way home. I didn't know that they caught my friend, Heaven. They slaughtered and killed her. Then they bagged her up and took her away, but I didn't know. I was too scared to look back, and I was running for my life.

"The next day, the people were looking for Heaven but didn't find her. Some people of the tribe thought she wandered off and got lost. They searched and looked everywhere, but she could not be found. I was too scared to tell anyone about what really happened. I might get in trouble, I thought. I forced myself to forget what happened that night the little people took her away. I have never seen her since, and I don't remember what she looked like. But I will never forget the little people. They looked like a goblin and an elf put together. But I still miss my friend, to this day."

"While we are on the subject of telling stories, I know one as well," said the Orphan. His parents were killed in a war with the Spanish when he was just a child. He had been on his own ever since. He was married with children and even had grandchildren of his own.

"The story begins when I first met my wife. We were so young, but I was a man, big-hearted and strong-willed. It was the day before I got married, and my friends were having a party in my honor. The party was big and wild. I had a great time. It was afterward, on my way home, that I ran into someone I'd never seen or met. He stood tall and muscular. He had long hair, and he was wearing a bandana on his head. It was dark, so I could not see the rest of his features. He walked and talked with me for a while. He asked me several questions like my name, where I was going, and where I was coming from. I said, 'My people call me the Orphan. I was coming from a party my friends put on for me, and I was on my way home.'

"'Where was the party?' he asked.

"'Just a few yards back.' I pointed with my lips in the direction I had come. The stranger asked, 'Where is your home?' I answered, 'Over there, where all the tepees are.' The stranger asked, 'What was the party for?' I told him I was getting married.

"He asked another question: 'Is your girlfriend beautiful?' I answered yes. He asked, 'Would you fight for her?' I said yes. He asked, 'Would you die for her?' I said, 'Yes, I would. What's with all these questions?' The stranger answered, 'I know your wife-to-be.

She is beautiful.' I said thank-you. Without hesitation, he said, 'I'll fight you for her.' I was shocked and I said, 'What! Are you kidding?' He answered, 'No, I am serious.' I said no, but then he kicked me and said, 'Yes, defend your future wife's honor.' His motions and punches were fast. I felt punches on my rib cage. I don't know what he hit me with, but I was bleeding. Instead of getting scared, I got mad, and I hit him with all my strength. It may have been minutes, but it seemed that we fought for a long time. I was able to pin him down to the ground on his stomach. We were both bleeding pretty bad. I grabbed him by his chin and on one side of his head, and was about to break his neck when, there under his bandana, I saw horns! They looked like little horns from a goat. I got scared and jumped off just as he said, 'I give up.' He got up and ran, making the sound of a horse galloping. I too ran all the way home, not looking back, not even once. For the first time in my life, I was truly scared.

"The next day, I went back to where I got into the fight with this thing. The place where we fought was torn up. The ground had prints of a cloven-hoofed beast besides my own, but I swear it was a man I fought. It had kicked me and put two holes in my ribs where it drove its hooves in. It stood as tall as a man. Someone said they heard it was half man and half goat. The top is man, and from the waist down it's a goat. He had little horns on his head, but you couldn't see them because he wore a bandana on his head to hide them. He usually comes out at night and early evenings. Other people have probably seen him but are too afraid to say anything."

The people looked astonished. Some of the young warriors said they would like to fight this half-man half-goat if they ever run into it. The Orphan told them, "It would kill you, any one of you, because it is strong. It is stronger than any one of you young warriors." One warrior said, "You got away from it, and you even put it to the ground." "Yes," said the Orphan, "but I am the strongest in our tribe." "But—" one of the young warriors said. "Enough," said the Orphan. "It can bring a horse down with one kick, and besides, it is probably old by now. Remember, it happened when I was a young man."

"I guess we all had interesting lives when we were younger," said Little Beaver.

"Why? Do you have a story to tell us, Grandma?" asked Feather Plume. She was Little Beaver's granddaughter.

"Oh, do I have a story! I heard this story told by my mother when I was knee high to a grasshopper. She once knew this little old lady who lived with a little girl deep in the woods. The old lady was harmless. She was always nice to everyone, even those who were afraid of her. But everyone in the tribe liked the little white girl. She was cute, adorable, and perfectly innocent, and she was always helping the old lady with everyday chores. They were poor people.

"The little girl would play with other children whenever the old lady would bring her to the camp. The old lady would trade furs, beadwork, and other things the people would be interested in. The old lady was described as short and on the chubby side. She always wore black—a black dress, black hat, black veil that covered her face—and she carried a black basket. Her face was never seen by anyone except for the little girl. The old lady spoke our language quite well, but she did not sound like one of the people. The old lady would always stay awhile and visit with the people. She was also a good cook. She spoke to the little girl in a strange language the people had never heard before, and the little girl responded the same way.

"The little girl, who was a blonde white girl, was Feather Plume's age. She was always dressed in beautiful dresses made from cloth the Indians had never seen before, and she wore long white stockings and shiny black shoes. The Apache children liked the way the little white girl dressed. But looks can be deceiving.

"One time, some of our people walked the old lady and the little girl home. The little girl was not her daughter. She just helped the old lady. Well, what happened next was a mystery. The people who went, a man and a woman and two children, never came back. Everyone who went was not related. They all went as a show of appreciation. The two of our girls went because they were closest friends to the white girl, and an elder woman was a friend to the old lady. The warrior was a boyfriend to the Apache woman.

"A wide search for the four went on for four days, but they were never found. Some of the tribe's men stopped to ask the old lady and the little girl if they knew what happened to the four people who took them home. She replied, 'The last time I saw them was when I stepped into my log cabin and they were on their way home.'"

Little Beaver went on with her story. "And soon after, people from our tribe and other tribes started losing people. It almost started a war between tribes because they started blaming each other. One day my aunt when she was young was called upon by the old lady to visit awhile. She had one of the warriors go with her to watch over her. When they arrived at the old lady's house, she played with the little white girl. While the two girls played, the man from the tribe was at a distance in the woods, and he watched. When the two kids went inside, the warrior ran to the cabin to see if he could have a look inside. The old lady told the children it was time to eat, and told the girls to wash up. In the meantime, she set the table. While the two girls ate, the old lady went into the kitchen. The man went to another window to see what the old lady was doing. She was making soup. It smelled so good it made him hungry.

"The old lady asked the girls if the food was good. They both answered yes. Of course, she also asked in our language to the Apache girl. The old lady was cutting up meat and putting it in boiling water she had in a kettle over a fire. The fire was in a fireplace built out of rocks and mud in her kitchen. As she cut up the meat to put it in the kettle, the warrior wondered what kind of meat it was, if it was deer, elk, or bear. What did it matter? It smelled good.

"Suddenly, he heard a scream. He ran to the window to look inside where the girls were eating. There he saw an animal. It looked like a wolf. It had already eaten half of the little Indian girl. The warrior was going to run in and tell the old lady and the little girl to get out of the house. He grabbed his knife and was about to run in. Suddenly, he stopped. What did he see? He saw the old lady come in, and she called the wolf. When the wolf ran and sat by the old lady, the wolf slowly turned back into the little white girl. Then, the old lady started to butcher the remains of the little Indian girl. After they skinned the dead girl, she cut her up like the way you would cut up beef.

"What was even scarier was what he saw of the old lady. Under her black veil, she looked like she was dead already, decaying! Her face was that of a skeleton with skin. She was already dead or something like that. After seeing what they did to the young Indian girl, he began to realize what had happened to the rest of the people that were never found. 'This old lady and the little girl, are they for real?' he thought. Then he rushed off to tell the others of the tribe.

"As he ran, he could hear the old lady yell at her dog, or the little white girl, whichever she was, 'Go get him!' The wolf took off after the guy. He almost made it back to the camp, yelling, 'Wild animal, wild animal!' The wolf jumped him and clawed and took several bites out of him before it ran off into the woods. The people must have scared it off. The guy that was attacked lived for a few days longer, long enough to tell the people what he saw and what must have happened to the other people. His wounds were too deep, and he slowly bled to death."

A voice called out from the crowd asking, "Did a group of warrior men go to where the old lady lived?" "Yes," Little Beaver said, "but no one was there. It looked as if no one ever lived there. I heard this story when I was a little girl."

At this time, everyone started back to their teepees. As they were leaving, they talked to each other about the stories they had just heard. But this was long ago.

Chapter Two

Modern Times

An age of brick houses, TVs, microwave ovens, CDs, DVDs, and cell phones and computers. An age of planes, trains, and cars, and most tribal members live on the reservation, and the children go to school, and most people have jobs, with satellite dishes on the roofs and four-by-four pickups in the driveways. The stories told long ago by their ancestors are told today. Stories told generation to generation by family, friends, and other relatives. Kids of today heard the stories and thought they were cool to listen to, but never believed in them.

It all started one summer, a week after Memorial Day. A group of children about ten of them, five boys and five girls, went camping for a couple of days. It was just as the sun was setting when the kids set out for their camping trip. They all had backpacks and sleeping bags, and they all brought their own food and water. Of the five boys, two were brothers, twins named Mark and Kyle. They were friends with the three other boys, whose names were Jon, Tim, and Francis. They were all friends with the girls, Julia, Mandan, Stacie, Geri, and Meredith. No relation, they were all friends and went to middle school together.

After hiking up into the mountains for about an hour, they stopped and set up camp. The boys slept in one big-sized tent that the twins brought. The girls slept in another tent that Mandan and Stacie brought.

Jon made a fire and said, "I hope y'all brought yourself enough food and water." Everyone replied yes. Geri said, "I hope someone brought toilet paper." Everyone looked at each other. Meredith said, "Aw, no!" Francis said, "That sucks. It's going to be a long night, people." But Geri was usually a nice person and would share the toilet paper if anyone needed it. Two people, Francis and Julia, brought cell phones for emergencies. They all ate and sat around the campfire in silence. Then they heard off in the distance the cries of coyotes and the whistle of a couple of bull elks. The girls screamed and huddled together, and the boys just laughed. Kyle said, "It's just coyotes and an elk or two. What's there to be afraid of?" Then Mark got the idea of Big Foot and told everyone that he roamed these woods at night. They all talked about whether he was real or not, and how different people had seen him around the rez.

That's when all the stories came about once more, just as they were back in the days of their great grandfathers. The stories of Big Foot; of the little men who were only seen during the evening; of Goat Man, the name he was given by children; and of the sweet old lady and the little white girl who lived with her.

As they laughed and scared each other into the night, they fell off to sleep one by one. Francis and Julia were the last ones up and still talking. They were talking about school, homework, tests, sports, parents, who was going out with who, and never mind, they fell asleep before talking about sex, but it was on their minds. The two were the oldest, both fourteen years old and in the eighth grade. Neither was dating, or that's what they told each other.

It was a little after 3 a.m. when Francis crawled into his sleeping bag in the tent. That night, he didn't think about the stories that were told. He just thought about Julia and wondered if she thought about him and, more importantly, if she liked him.

The next morning, everyone was awakened by the twins trying to start a fire. They were arguing about who could start one, calling each other "girls" or using racial slurs.

Geri was first to come out of the girls' tent. Her hair was every which way but straight. The boys laughed at her. She said, "Go to hell." Then she woke up Meredith and said, "Go with me." "Where?"

Meredith asked. "To the restroom," said Geri. "Out here?" said Meredith. "Do you see restroom facilities out here?" "Shut up and let's go," said Geri. Jon said, "Don't forget to wipe." All the boys laughed. "At least we wipe!" said Geri, flipping the finger.

The girls went into the forest away from camp. The camp was nestled right in the middle of the big pine trees. The tree branches had green, stringy moss hanging. The ground was covered with oak bushes and in all that was a bald spot where the camp was made, up away from civilization.

"I could live up here," Mandan said, crawling out of her tent. Then she asked where Geri and Meredith were. "Big Foot ate them last night," Kyle said. "Oh, shut up," said Mandan. Julia and Stacie were up now.

Suddenly, a loud scream was heard in the distance, and Meredith came running back. Tim asked, "What is it?" Meredith said, "I saw something dead, not too far from here." All the boys except Jon ran in the direction Meredith was pointing. They ran and suddenly stopped. Tim yelled, "How far?" Geri yelled back, "Look for our footprints." The boys followed and stopped. Tim yelled again, "One of you guys sure take big ones!"

Mark said, "It's only a dead dog. That's no big deal." Kyle asked, "How did a dog get all the way up here? Why was the dog up here to begin with?" Mark said, "I don't know."

"And look," Kyle said, "there's a rope around its neck and legs. And what about this tin axe? It's the length of my hand! These ropes are a little bigger than a shoestring." Francis said, "This is a little freaky." Just then the girls came running up to the boys. Julia asked, "What is it?" Tim said, "It's just a dead dog. Where is Jon?" "He stayed back to watch over the camp," said Julia. "Look at this little hatchet," said Francis. Mandan said, "What's the big deal about a hatchet?" Mark said, "It's the size of my hand, you idiot."

"Well, I don't know how big a hatchet is, asshole. And don't call me an idiot," said Mandan.

Mark said, "I'm taking this little axe." "It probably belongs to one of Jon's G.I. Joe dolls," said Geri. "After all, he is the youngest." "No, this looks real. The head is steel," said Tim.

Then Geri said, "You guys probably planned this, huh? Trying to scare us. Well, I'm not afraid of a dead dog." "Who screamed when you were taking a dump, then?" said Kyle. Geri and Meredith both looked at Kyle and said "shut up" at the same time. "You suck," said Geri. Francis said, "We didn't plan anything. Come on. Let's go back to the campsite before Jon gets scared and starts to cry."

"If you think you can scare us into sleeping in the same tent with you guys, you're crazy," said Mandan. Although she knew she would feel safer, she also knew the twins were perverts, so she said nothing more.

They all arrived at the camp just to find Jon playing around with the campfire. Francis yelled, "Hey, you little fag, what are you doing?" Jon said, "Nothing." Mark handed the axe to Jon, saying, "Here's a toy for you and your G.I. Joe doll." Jon said, "Cool, it feels like a real axe." Meanwhile, Stacie was making noise in the tent by moving stuff around. "What are you doing?" said Julia. "I'm making sure that little fart didn't go through our stuff," said Stacie.

Francis asked, "What are you girls going to do today?" "We wanna go here and there, check out this and that," said Geri.

Geri was an average seventh grader. She could be a real smart ass. She got it from her mom, but most of the time she was kind and generous. She wore clothes that captured the eye of any boy around her. She had one sister and two brothers. She was the youngest of her family.

Francis said, "Go where you all want I don't care."

Francis was an athlete in school and usually got by on his wits for classes. He was an only child but learned early on how to earn what he wanted from his parents.

So everyone was leaving except for Jon and Julia. Jon was a sixth grader but was supposed to be in the fifth. Because he was smart, he was moved ahead one grade. They all lived in one area, a few houses apart. So he was not counted out, nor was Stacie. She was the youngest of the girls, by age not grade. She was half white. Her dad was a tribal member and her mom was white. She could be a child or a grown-up, but she was mostly a child around Jon when they played together, or a young grown-up around Mandan.

Mandan was not only Stacie's best friend, but lived next door to her. They did everything together. Mandan was a wild girl who came from a broken home. Both of her parents drank and didn't care for Mandan. Mandan's dad was white, and her mother was a Tribal member like all the parents of all her friends. But Mandan and Stacie went away to school every school year, and they did not act like native children. They acted like white girls. And all the children called them city girls or white girls.

The twins, Mark and Kyle, had a crush on Mandan and Stacie but were too shy to tell them. The twins lived in a two-story house and shared everything. They had everything the same, except Mark had a four-wheeler and Kyle had a dirt bike. They came from a respectable family who went to church every Sunday. It's a wonder why they were perverts.

Meredith was the one with the most common sense. She was mentally average but lived by her lores. She grew up fast on the inside, but on the outside, she was still a child of thirteen years old. A thirteen-year-old like Tim, but Tim was the brains of the bunch. He liked his friends, even though they called him a nerd. Sometimes he lived in a world of logic, so he never understood girls, but he was fascinated with them. He also couldn't grasp the know-how of being impractical.

And there was Julia, a rich girl, or a spoiled brat nevertheless. She was the oldest of the girls. She had whatever she wanted, but she was not snobby like other rich girls in school. Those girls were white, and she did not care too much for white girls.

Julia said she would stay at camp and babysit Jon. Jon returned the gesture by flipping the finger, and Julia laughed.

Mark said, "We're going now. Try not to molest Jon, OK?"

"Screw you," said Julia.

While Julia talked on her cell phone and Jon played with his little hatchet, everyone went out and about. The twins went back to where they had found the dead dog only to discover that it was gone.

"What happened to it?" asked Mark. "I dunno. Maybe coyotes or a bear dragged it off someplace," said Kyle. "Or it was picked up and taken somewhere," said Mark. "Maybe the people who killed the dog with their little tools ran off with it." "Yeah, with Santa Claus," said Kyle. "Shut up. I'm serious," Mark said. Meanwhile, the girls were attempting to climb to the top of the mountain from where they were camping while they talked about boys and gossiped about other girls. Mandan said, "We should have brought some beer or something good to drink." Meredith said, "Is that all you care about, is drinking?" "Yeah," Stacie said. "Chicken?" asked Mandan. "No," said Stacie. Geri said, "How about you get drunk and we leave you up here?" "Like you would," said Mandan.

"What do you think the guys are doing?" asked Mandan.

"They're probably playing with bugs or something," said Geri.

Francis and Tim were already at the top of the mountain. "Look at our community down there," said Francis, pointing to the bottom of the mountain. "I'll bet the girls get lost and we end up looking for them," said Tim.

"Hey, look, deer tracks. Or are they elk?" said Tim. "Dunno," said Francis. "Looks like it was a whole herd, from the looks of things. That reminds me of the story of Goat Man," he added. "Goat Man?" asked Tim. "Yeah, he's half goat and half man," said Francis. "Which part of him is which?" asked Tim. "From the waist up is a man and the bottom part is a goat. But that is an old story from a long time ago," said Francis.

Tim said, "I never heard of him. I only heard of Big Foot, but then who hasn't?" "Do you believe in Big Foot?" asked Francis. Tim said, "No, do you?" Francis said, "No. They're just stories to scare little kids so they won't stay out late at night." Tim asked, "If you saw either one right now, what would you do?" "I'd take a stand and fight to show them who's boss of the rez," Francis said. "Really?" asked Tim. "Naw, just kidding. I wouldn't know what to do," said Francis. "How about you?" Tim said, "I'd run and get the hell out of here!" They both laughed.

While Francis and Tim talked about Big Foot and Goat Man, back at camp Julia was trying to get to know what kind of person Jon was. She was asking him questions he didn't care for or didn't know how to answer. Julia asked, "Jon, do you have a girlfriend? Do you like any of the girls who came on the campout?" He answered no to every question. He liked Stacie only as a friend because they were playmates. "Do you have any questions for me?" asked Julia. "No," Jon said. "Can I see your axe?" she asked. Jon said, "Here," and he gave it to her. She gazed at it and thought to herself how real it looked and wondered if it was really made by someone who lived up here.

"Is there more of these people?"

"Do you like it?" Jon said. "Yeah, I think it looks pretty cool," Julia said. She gave the little axe back to Jon. He started playing again. Meanwhile, her mind wandered. "Is there other people up here? Who lives here? I wonder if they're nice, or do they simply kill anything alive?" she wondered.

Just as the girls were nearing the top of the mountain, they came across a hideaway, a place made from bushes tied together with twine. Old blankets and clothes were on the ground inside. Bones and fur from different kinds of animals were scattered about. It had the smell of rotting animals, moldy clothes, human body odor, and bad breath all rolled into one smell.

Just as the girls were going to enter, Stacie gagged and said, "It stinks in here." "You big baby, I'll go in," said Geri. But she could not stand the smell either. Meredith said, "Now who is the big baby?" "You go in there," said Geri. "No way. I'm staying right out here," said Meredith.

Mandan said, "I'm calling Francis and them." "You don't even know where they are," said Geri. Mandan started yelling and calling out loud, "Francis! Tim! Where are you guys?" After yelling a few minutes, the boys arrived, including the twins.

Tim asked, "What do you want? Did you guys get lost?" Mandan said, "No. Shut up and follow me." So they all went to where the hideaway was.

"What the hell," said Francis. "That looks cool," said Tim. "You think that's cool, go inside," said Geri. Tim went inside and then ran back out. "It smells in there! Whatever could smell so bad?" he asked.

As they all stood there gazing at it, wondering who or what made the hideaway, Stacie said, "Are we going to Julia and Jon?" Francis said, "We could tell Julia, but not Jon because—" Before Francis could say any more, Geri arid Stacie were already running toward the camp area calling Julia and Jon. "Forget that idea," Francis said.

Julia and Jon were sleeping when they heard their names being called. Jon was sleeping by a log he had been chopping on. Julia was asleep on a sleeping bag she'd unrolled on the ground. Jon called out, "Over here!" Julia stood up and said, "What is it? Did you guys see a bear?" "No, we have something to show you," said Stacie. "What is it? What is it?" Jon repeated. "Come and follow us," said Geri.

They finally arrived at the hideaway. Julia said, "Wow. It looks kinda neat. Who made it?" "We don't know," said Francis. "Look how they tied the tree branches together to make a rooftop," said Tim. Jon said, "Man, it stinks in there." "Well, whoever built it would probably be mad if we messed with it," said Kyle. Mark said, "Yeah."

Geri said, "Maybe it belongs to the people that killed the dog Meredith and I saw this morning. They'll probably kill us too if we mess with their home." "You're such an idiot," said Francis. "Don't you think if this was their home, they would be here?" Julia said, "Yeah, but what if they're out hunting?" Tim said, "What if it belongs to Big Foot?" "Big Foot?" said Stacie with fear in her eyes. "I'm scared," she said. "Me, too," said Jon.

"There! Are you satisfied? You scared the hell out of both of them," said Francis. "Me? I'm not the one talking about Big Foot and hunters who might be killers living up here in the woods," said Geri. "All right, everyone. Shut up and let's go back to the camp," said Meredith. "Why?" asked Francis. "Just 'cause Jon and Stacie are all of a sudden scared? Give me a break," he said. "Me, too," said Tim.

Mandan said, "I thought we came up here to get away from our parents and do what we wanted and have fun." Geri said, "Yeah, let's go see what else we can find." So Jon, Stacie, and Julia returned to the campsite. Jon and Stacie were terrified of what might have made the hideaway. Julia went back to the camp because she knew someone had to watch over Jon and Stacie. Julia called Francis on the cell phone and said, "I'm watching Jon and Stacie here at the camp, so you keep an eye on the rest."

"Why me?" he asked. "Because you're the oldest. Be a man, will ya?" said Julia. "Shut up," Francis said, and he hung up.

Mark said, "OK, how about the girls go one way and the boys go the other?" "I guess you're going with the girls," said Kyle. Geri said, "I'd rather have Mark go with us than you," pointing at Kyle. "Right, Mandan?" "Right," she said. "You two are so dumb," said Meredith. "They're identical twins. What's the difference?" So everyone went exploring about and found nothing more until it was evening.

Everyone was back at camp. Once more the twins were at it again, trying to make a fire. "It will be morning before you guys start a fire," said Francis. Jon said, "It would be cool to roast hotdogs tonight." "Yeah, let me pull 'em out of my backpack," said Geri. "Leave him alone," said Tim.

"I have twenty dollars, if someone wants to go down to the store and buy some hotdogs," said Julia. Francis said, "Mark and Kyle, you two should go, and I'll stay and watch over everyone a here."

Kyle said, "Why the hell should we go?" Then Francis said, "'Cause if you don't, I'll kick your ass." "That's good enough reason for me," said Mark. "Let's go, Kyle." "You wimp," said Kyle to Mark as they were leaving.

The twins made it to the store and bought some hotdogs, buns, and some Cokes. At the small convenience store, Mr. Meens was the owner. He was a white man, but he was always nice to all in the community. He was tall and a little on the heavy side, with a bald spot at the top of his head. He wore glasses. He always wore button-down shirts, dress pants that were held up by suspenders, and regular, everyday shoes. He was a nice man.

Mr. Meens asked, "What are you boys up to? You guys going on a weenie roast?" The twins looked at each other and laughed. "No," said Mark, "we're going camping."

"Well, you boys be careful. You don't want to end up like Patrick," said Mr. Meens.

"Patrick who?" asked Kyle. "Patrick Larson, the high school basketball player," said Mr. Meens. "Why? What happened to him?" asked Mark. "He died. He was found dead this morning. He was ripped to shreds and torn apart. There are pieces of him missing, like his legs, hands, and a big piece of his back was cut open and the insides were taken out. It's got the police and FBI all baffled," said Mr. Meens. "That's pretty messed up," said Mark. "We'll be careful, and we'll tell the others," said Kyle. "You boys have a good day and be careful," said Mr. Meens.

The twins decided to go by the Larsons' house before returning to the camp. Mrs. Larson looked very upset, and she looked as though she'd been crying. There were a lot of people at her house. Mr. Larson was talking to some of the neighbors, saying he wished he knew who killed his son. "I will make them pay for what they did," he said. He was very angry. Mark said, "Let's go. I've had enough."

The twins started back up the mountain. Neither one spoke the whole time. When they got back to the camp, everyone was laughing and having a good time. They saw the look on the twins' faces. Mandan asked, "What's wrong? You guys look like you've just seen a ghost." "You look like you came from a funeral," said Geri. "I think we did," said Mark. "What are you talking about?" asked Julia. Mark was not eager to tell them.

Kyle said, "Do you guys remember Patrick Larson?" "Yeah, what about him?" asked Meredith. "Well, he . . . ," Mark could not say the words. "Well, he, uh, what?" asked Francis. "He died," said Kyle. "His body was found today. It was ripped to pieces, and pieces of his body were taken away." "That's a lie!" said Geri. "No, it's true! Mr. Meens told us, and there were a lot of cars at the Larsons' house, and Mr. Larson said that he will make them pay for what they did to Patrick," Mark said.

"Don't you guys think we should go back home and show our respect?" asked Julia. "For what? We didn't really know Patrick anyway," said Francis. "I mean, he really didn't talk to any of us. He surely didn't hang out with us. I mean, to me, he was just a high school jock who was a great basketball player."

"Yeah, let's continue with our campout and finish what we started, if that's OK with everyone else," said Tim. So everyone agreed and cooked their hotdogs and ate them and drank their Cokes. Everyone laughed and told jokes, but the death of a student weighed heavy on their minds because of his age and because he lived near to all of them.

Francis spoke up and said, "Before it gets dark, if anyone wants to go home, you'd better leave now. 'Cause I don't want to hear any crying or no one saying, 'I'm scared,' from any of you."

"Ooh, big man, way to take charge," said Mandan. Francis said, "Shut up, you bi—" Julia quickly interrupted, saying, "None of the girls are going back, right?" They all said "right." "How about you all?" asked Stacie. "No," said the boys at the same time. "You guys better not scare us tonight," said Geri, "or we'll never speak to you again."

"Before we turn in, I want to ask a favor of you guys," said Julia. "The answer is yes. Y'all can sleep by us in the same tent," said Mark. "Not that, you perverts," said Julia. "I want to know if one of you guys can go with us in case we need the restroom or anything else. After all, we are all just friends, right? And we respect each other's—" she said. "Yeah, yeah," said Francis, "we get you. You don't have to say any more."

As they watched the fire into the night, they all had different thoughts on their minds. Slowly, they all turned in, one by one, until it was once again Julia and Francis who were the last ones up. Julia wanted to ask questions about the hideaway, but not in front of everyone else. Now that they were alone, she thought it was a good time to ask. She said, "Hey." "What?" he said.

"What do you think about the little axe and that hideout-looking thing we saw today?" asked Julia. "Nothing," said Francis, adding, "Why? Got you scared?" "No, baffled, more like it," answered Julia, yawning. "I'm tired." Lying back, she said, "Look at the stars. There must be a million of 'em?" She sat up and looked at Francis and smiled.

Then she heard something. "What is that?" she asked. Francis said, "I don't know." Then they saw someone standing a few yards from them. "Oh, shit, it's Big Foot," said Francis. "It can't be," said Julia. It came closer and closer until it appeared in the light of the fire. "Oh, my God, it's Patrick Larson!" screamed Julia. She continued to scream, "Leave me alone! Leave me alone!"

"Wake up! Wake up!" shouted Francis, shaking her by the shoulders. She opened her eyes, scared stiff. She grabbed for Francis and clung onto him. "It's all right. You just had a bad dream," said Francis. "You must have dozed off when you lay back and left me talking to myself." He asked, "What were you dreaming about?" She said, "It was the guy who died, Patrick. I was dreaming he came to me here at the camp and grabbed me. And I got scared. I was screaming for someone to help me."

"You screamed, all right, and loud too! I'm surprised you didn't bring the sun up," said Francis. "Did I wake anyone up?" asked Julia. "Obviously not," said Francis. "Those guys could sleep through a war!"

That night, Julia slept by Francis by the fire. Just before dawn, Francis woke her up and said, "You better get back into your tent before anyone wakes up." So Julia went into her tent, and Francis went into his. None of the girls heard Julia come in. Francis crawled into his sleeping bag, and just as he got comfortable, Tim laughed a little and said to him, "Did you get a little?" Francis didn't say anything and went off to sleep.

It was late in the morning and getting hot. Jon was running around and yelling, "It's time to get up! We're going home today." "Will you shut up, you little shit. I wanna sleep more," said Geri. Mark said, "Let's build a fire." "No, we don't need to. Besides, we're leaving soon," said Kyle. It was almost noon when everybody was finally up, sleeping bags rolled up, tents packed away, and everyone's clothes put away in backpacks of their own.

"Let's go," said Tim. "Let's get the hell out of here and go home. I'm starving." Jon said, "Finally we're leaving. I'm so hungry I could eat a horse!" "You smell like one," said Mandan. "Shut up," Jon answered.

Down the mountain they all went. No one was wasting time. They all talked about what they were going to do when they got home. Arriving in the areas of the houses where they lived, each one of them went to their house. Mandan went to Stacie's house with her.

Geri, on her way home, said to Meredith, "Call me later." The twins walked home, arguing as usual. Everyone went their own way as if their friendship was at an end.

Chapter Three

Back Home

A few minutes after unpacking, Francis's cell phone rang. It was Julia on the other end.

"Hello," he said. "Are you going to the funeral tomorrow?" she asked. "I hate funerals," Francis said. "I have to," said Julia. "My mom and dad are going." "We're not going, and I'm not gonna go, either," said Francis. "Is anyone else going?" she asked. Francis answered, "I don't know. You might be the only one out of all of us who's going." "Shit, that sucks," said Julia. "Gotta go. See ya," Francis said, and he hung up. Julia said "bye" to no sound.

A few days went by, and everything was running normal, kids playing till the sun went down. Mandan ran down the street to tell her she had news, but Stacie had already heard the news. Mandan asked, "Did you hear about Mrs. Anderson's little boy?" Stacie answered, "Yes, I heard it on the news." "Was his name Chuck?" asked Mandan.

"Yeah, everyone called him Chucky. How old was he?" asked Stacie. "I think he was five years old. Remember, he used to ride his bike up and down the street you live on," answered Mandan. "I know. It's scary," said Stacie.

Just then, Tim and the twins went skateboarding by Stacie's house. "Hey, babes, what's up?" asked Tim. "Some more bad news," replied Stacie. "Who?" asked Mark. "When?" asked Kyle.

"It was that little boy Chucky," replied Mandan, "last night."

"Holy shit, what happened to him?" asked Tim. "No one knows. It's like he disappeared. Most of the town people and police went looking for him," said Stacie.

"Who'd want to kidnap that little guy anyway?" asked Mark. "Maybe a pervert or a frag," said Tim, pointing to the twins, and Mandan added, "Like you two. One gay and the other a pervert." "Screw you," said Mark.

"Maybe one of you guys stole Chucky and did something with him," said Mandan. Tim interrupted, "Will you shut up? This is serious, guys. The police are still investigating Patrick's murder." Then Tim and the twins left.

The cell phone rang, and Mandan answered. It was Geri. "Hey, girl, what's up? Yeah, we all heard the news. Where you at? Well, come over to Stacie's house. No one else except Stacie. OK? See ya." "What did she say?" asked Stacie. "The same. If we heard the news on Chucky," replied Mandan.

"I wonder if he walked off too far somewhere and got lost," said Stacie. "Or do you think he really got kidnapped?"

"Come on, on the rez? You think that would happen here?" asked Mandan. "Nowadays, anything is possible," replied Stacie.

Geri rode up on a horse, saying, "Hey, girls, wanna go for a ride? Maybe we can help the search party look for that little boy." "No," said Stacie, "I think I'll hang out at home." "I'll hang out with you," said Mandan. Stacie told Geri, "You can stay too, if you want," and Geri replied, "I guess I can hang out with y'all for a little while." She got off her horse and tied it to the old junk car that was on the side of the house.

Tim and the twins arrived at Francis's house to find Francis on the porch practicing with his electric guitar. "I didn't know you played," said Tim. "Yeah, but I still need a lot of practice. After all, all practice makes perfect, right?" replied Francis.

"Hey, did you hear what happened to Chucky?" asked Tim. "Yeah. What about it?" said Francis. "Nothin'," said Tim. "Then why ask?" said Francis. "Just wondered, I guess," said Tim.

Francis said, "I'm not related to him, so I don't have any concerns about him." "What about your friends?" asked Tim. "What about them?" replied Francis. "What if it was one of us? You know, your bros," said Tim. "Well, it's not, so I'm not worried about it. OK? So chill. Quit worrying about it. You act just like my mom sometimes," said Francis.

"Hey, what are you two blabbing about like two old ladies?" Tim asked the twins. Mark said, "We had an idea." "Yeah, we thought about the hideout we found when we went camping," said Kyle. "What about it?" asked Tim. "What if the kidnappers stashed that little boy there? Maybe we should check," said Kyle. "Maybe you should check by yourself and get attacked by whoever made that hideout," said Tim, "and maybe you wouldn't be coming back either, and you'll end in the same place as Chucky."

"Oh, blow it out your ass. No one was talking to you anyway," said Kyle. "Besides, I wouldn't ask you to go with us to check." "Yeah, so why don't you shut up before I knock your face off?" said Mark. Tim shouted, "Why don't you try it!" They looked face to face and waited for the other to strike first, then pushed each other, but nothing more. Kyle and Francis knew they wouldn't hit each other. They were all friends and had their arguments and disagreements, but they never hurt each other, no matter how bad the situation got. The girls were the same way with each other.

Francis said, "Hey, guys, knock it off, or I'll beat the shit out of both of you." They both looked at Francis and each other and backed down. Kyle asked Mark, "Are you ready?" and Mark replied, "Yeah, let's go."

"Hold on, guys. I wanna go with you," said Francis. "I thought you weren't concerned," remarked Tim. "I'm not, but it's boring around here. There's nothing to do," said Francis. "You wanna bring Jon?" asked Tim. "No, not this time," replied Francis. "Besides, if we really found that little boy, Jon's liable to freak out." "OK, let's go. Do you guys remember where it's at?" asked Tim. Mark answered, "We just go to the campsite and hang a right."

So they were off and running, in a hurry to get up the mountain. They first had to run past Stacie's house to the end of the street, which came to a court drive, then through the oak brushes up the mountain. After they had run a long way, they heard Mandan and Geri calling out to them, "Hey, where y'all going?"

"We're going back to where we were camping," replied Tim. Mandan asked, "For what?" "Actually, we want to find the hideout," Francis answered. Mandan asked if they could go too, and Tim replied, "Sure, come on. Who else is coming?" Mandan replied, "Everybody but Stacie. She's already freaked out about that little boy. She don't need any more trauma in her life." So they all ran to where they were camped several days ago.

Mark asked with a look of confusion, "Which way?" Tim replied, "Go right," but Geri said, "No, it's straight up the mountain from the campsite." So that's where they went. They came upon the hideaway, and forgetting how bad it smelled inside, they come out gagging and holding their noses. "Oh shit," said Francis, "I forgot how bad that smelled." "You ain't lying," said Tim.

Meredith grabbed a long stick and picked up some clothes from inside the hideaway. She said, "Hey, look, guys!" On the end of the stick were a small white T-shirt pair of blue jeans. One Nike shoe lay on the ground. "You don't suppose this belongs to that little boy Chucky, do you?" asked Meredith. Francis said, "Just leave it there in the hideout, and when we find out for sure what he was wearing, we'll tell the police."

Geri said, "If his clothes are here, where is he at?" Francis responded, "Like I said, let's go get some info on what that little boy was wearing. Then I think we should let the police worry about where he might be." Tim, concerned, replied, "Whatever. Let's go." They all ran back down the mountain and to Chucky's house.

Tim asked, "Who is going to ask his mom, Mrs. Anderson?" Kyle replied, "I will, but I go by myself so she won't suspect anything." "Good idea," replied Mandan. "We'll wait at my house. Try to get as much info as you can." Kyle asked, "Why? I thought we were gonna leave it up to the police." "There's nothing wrong with getting a little extra info," replied Mandan. "Now, go!" Kyle walked to the Anderson's house and knocked on the door but got no answer.

The Andersons lived in a house run by the HUD, like most families on the reservation. Others lived in trailers that they bought themselves. The houses were fifty to a hundred yards apart. It looked like the projects, only in wide, open range. There were some families who had their own homes, but they worked off the reservation.

The reservation was roughly a hundred square miles, with a population of two thousand people. They were a tribe of forgotten Indians. They called themselves Grey Stalk. In their community were eight hundred houses, not including trailers scattered about the community. A casino, a small fifty-room hotel, one convenience store, one grocery store, a gas station, and an old renovated building for a Boys & Girls Club were all along one main street that ran off the highway. There was also an elementary, middle, and high school, all in separate buildings, but all small. The community sat at the base of the mountain. The mountain was part of a mountain range that ran through a big part of the reservation. Their community was in the open range, for expansion. The administration offices were in a small building behind the casino. There were bear paws with claws on front and at the end of the printed word "Administration." There was also a helipad for emergencies and a police station.

From the Anderson's house to Mandan's was a quarter of a mile walk. Kyle returned to find everyone waiting, sitting on the front porch. "Well, what did she say?" asked Mandan. "There's no one home," replied Kyle. Geri asked, "Did you knock on the door?" "Stupid! Yeah, I did," answered Kyle. Julia said, "We should just wait and see what happens."

They all saw Stacie and Jon rollerblading down the street. Stacie said, "Let's see what everyone's doing at Mandan's house." Jon replied, "OK," and they both arrived to see why everyone was at Mandan's except them.

Tim asked, "Are you rollerblading with your chick, huh, Jon?" Jon replied, "At least I have one. You're so ugly no one likes you." Everyone laughed; then Tim said, "Shut up, all of you." Francis said, "Maybe you should keep your mouth shut next time." Stacie asked, "Why are you all here?" Mandan replied, "We're just hanging out and waiting to see if we hear anything else on Chucky. What are you two doing?" Stacie replied, "We were bored, so we decided to go rollerblading."

Just then Officer Sicord came by to tell the kids about what happened and not to be alone. The officer was half white and half Indian from another tribe. No one ever knew which tribe, because he never told anyone. He was one officer of many who worked for law enforcement for the tribe.

"Hey, y'all want something from the store?" asked Julia. "I'm buying." Tim said eagerly, "Hell, yeah, man. It's hot today." Julia said, "Well, you don't have to cuss. Remember, the police said to stick together when we go somewhere." They walked to the store, talking about what they wanted.

The store was half a mile from Mandan's house, but on a hot day of ninety-five degrees with no breeze, it seemed like a mile and two feet from hell. Finally, getting to the store, they all walked in and headed for the soda and ice cream. Meredith said, "Hi, Mr. Means," and Mr. Means replied, "Hi, kids. What are you all doing on this fine day?" Stacie said, "It's too hot to be a fine day!"

They were all putting their Cokes and ice cream on the counter while Mr. Means rang it up. Then they saw a woman dressed in black, but they could not see her face. Jon asked, "Who is that, Mr. Means? Is that your wife?" Mr. Means answered, "No, I hired her yesterday. She works for me now. She has a daughter somewhere around here. Hey, why don't you kids walk by and say hi to her?" Stacie asked, "What's her name?" and Mr. Means replied, "Her name is Olga."

They all walked by in a straight line, saying, "Hi, Olga," and introducing themselves, except Geri. Geri said that Olga gave her the creeps. Mandan added, "Me, too, but we should try to be nice anyway." Olga said hi in return. Her voice sounded old and shaky. Her face could not be seen.

The kids left the store. "Good-bye, Mr. Means," said the girls. "Later, dude," said Francis, and the rest of the boys added, "Later." Jon said, "Good-bye, Mr. Means," and Mr. Means replied, "I'll see you kids later. Be careful, after all that's happened these past few days." He thought to himself, *We had two people that died already.* Still thinking, he said out loud, "I guess there could be one more person that's gonna die." Just then the lady in black, who was cleaning, looked up at him and said, "It could be one of us, don't you think?" Mr. Meens went about his business and said nothing to her.

Meanwhile, the kids were walking back to Mandan's house. Tim said, "I wonder what that lady's daughter looks like." Geri replied, "Probably mean and ugly."

Francis said, "Let's go to our cheap, little park." Tim replied, "Yeah, you can tell the tribe put a lot of money into it." Mark added, "We have a casino, and this is the best our tribe can do?" Julie said, "Shut up and be glad you get a dividend once a year." Tim said, "Just 'cause you're rich, rich girl who lives on the rez!" Julia responded, "I'm not rich. My parents are." Tim said, "Oh, I forgot you're a brat."

Evening time was approaching, and the bunch was sitting at the park when the police came by. Jon said, "Hey, look, it's Officer Beckman." Officer Beckman warned the kids, "Don't stay out too late. We don't want any more happening around here." Geri asked, "Did you find Chucky or anything on him?" "No," Officer Beckman said, "we're still searching. We got the majority of the rez looking for him. Don't you all worry, we'll find him." Tim said to himself, *Yeah, dead somewhere.*

Officer Beckman added, "Well, you kids have fun now, and remember, don't stay out too late." He drove off with concern. After all, he was one of the police on duty that night if something happened to them. *I was last to see them*, he thought. *I don't know if I can handle that. I better go back and just tell them all to go home right now.* When he got there, the kids were gone. *Oh, good*, he thought, and drove off.

Chapter Four

The Next Day

Mr. Meens was cleaning the doormat outside his doorway. A police car drove up. Mr. Meens said, "Good morning, Vern. You going on duty?" Vern answered, "Yeah. Thought I'd get a cup of coffee before I went on patrol."

Mr. Meens asked, "I know it's police business, but I'm concerned for that little boy who was taken a couple of days ago. You got any leads?" Vern replied, "No. We looked everywhere around here and cannot find him. And no one saw anything. The last thing Mrs. Anderson remembered is her son playing outside just after sundown."

Mr. Meens asked, "Do y'all have enough help? I mean, you still have to find out who killed Patrick, don't you?" Vern answered, "Yes, we're still looking into it. This is the first time we've had a murder and a kidnapping here on the rez. Our usual jobs are spousal abuse, people passing out by the highway, DWI, and underage drinking. But the FBI is handling the murder situation, so we can go about our usual business. This sure is good coffee."

Mr. Meens replied, "Thank you. My new employee made it. Come say hi to Olga. Hey, Olga, can you come here for a sec?" Olga came over and said, "Good morning, Officer." Vern responded, "Good morning to you, too. How are you on this fine day?" Olga replied, "I do well, thank you. I want you to meet my daughter. Her name is Teri. She's friends with that girl down the street named Lisa."

Vern said, "I know her and her family. They're very nice. I think you'll like them. Are you going to school here, Teri?"

Teri answered, "I sure hope so, 'cause I wanna go to school with my new friend." Vern added, "I hope you get more than just one friend," and Teri replied, "Me too. I'm gonna go play now, OK?" Vern told her, "Sure, go ahead. I best finish my coffee and hit the road."

Mr. Meens's store was usually the place to go for coffee and to pick up a few pastry goods or doughnuts. On occasion, he would sell breakfast burritos packed with potatoes, eggs, and a choice of Spam, bacon, beans, sausage, or ham. He always sold out on burritos.

Olga worked for Mr. Meens and did not demand a big pay. The two-bedroom house he provided and the food whenever she needed it was enough, but the money came in handy when it came time to buy clothes for Teri. Teri was a twelve-year-old in the sixth grade. She was white, but since her mom worked for Mr. Meens, who was an exception for the tribe, she would attend school on the rez when summer was over.

Teri was friends with Lisa Thomson, a girl the same age as her. Her father ran the gas station. His shop always had a car or a couple of four-wheelers in it that needed to be fixed. Mr. Thomson was always dirty and smelled like oil, except when he wasn't working at his station, which was on Sundays. He always took his family to church and then out to eat, so Lisa never played with Teri on Sundays.

Teri was considered the poorest girl in town. But she did have nice clothes going for her. No one knew much about her, except that her mom worked for Mr. Meens and they lived in a small house behind the store.

Lisa lived a mile from the store, but when you're used to walking everywhere in the community, it isn't that far to walk. Most other kids got around on horses or four-wheelers and an occasional dirt bike.

Once, Teri tried to get Lisa to go up into the mountains with her, but her parents wouldn't allow it. When Teri was alone, she often went up into the mountains without fear. Lisa had asked her, "Do you always go up into the mountains by yourself?" Teri had replied,

"Yeah. I have lots of fun up there. I can be wild and free and do what I want to. You should go with me sometimes." Lisa told her, "If my mom and dad would ever let me. I know some kids who go camping up there, but not all the time. Most of the time, they hang out around here." "Who are they?" Teri had asked. "I'd like to meet them sometime." Lisa told her she probably would, because they came to Mr. Meens to buy pop and chips and candy or ice cream, but she didn't know their names. "Where are they at usually?" asked Teri. Lisa told her, "They're usually down the other side on Main Street. The other side of the store."

Mr. Meens's store was right in the middle of everything. Main Street ran east to west. The highway was at the east end. The west side of the store was where most kids hung out. Teri said, "I hope I get to meet them one of these days." Lisa told her, "You will. After all, your mom works in the store they go to." Teri asked her, "Are any of them losers?" and Lisa answered, "I don't know, 'cause I never hung out with them. By the way, where did you guys come from?" Teri answered, "We came from another Indian reservation. It seems like a long time ago." Lisa asked, "Why did you leave?" Teri replied, "Problems and troubles that I'd rather not talk about. Hey, do you want an ice cream or something from the store?"

Lisa answered, "No, maybe later. Let's just play right here by the road and stay close to the store for now. I'll go home when my mom gets off from work." Teri asked, "Where is she?" and Lisa replied, "She works at the casino. She's one of those people that count money all day."

Just as they started to play, they heard the sound of horses on the road. Teri asked, "Who is that?" "I don't know," Lisa replied, "just somebody on horses." As the girls sat and watched to see who was riding, they heard girls talking and laughing. Geri was on one horse, and Mandan and Stacie were on the other, with Mandan sitting in front. They rode up to the side of the store and got off, tying their horses to a flagpole. They were out of Lisa's and Teri's sight. They walked around to the front of the store.

"Hi, Mr. Meens," Stacie said. Mr. Meens replied, "Hi, girls. What are you all up to, and where is the rest of the bunch?" Mandan answered, "I think the guys went fishing, and Julia and Meredith went shopping in Rio."

The city of Rio went by no other name. It was a suburb of an industrial city. Rio was thirty miles from Grey Stalk Reservation. It had a population of two hundred thousand people. It was a city of malls, theaters, night clubs, hospitals, and everything a city could have wanted or needed. It was a place where everyone from the reservation went for supplies, health care, food, or to just have a good time.

The girls each grabbed a pop, paid, and left. They came out and looked at the two girls sitting on the roadside. Mandan whispered, "Who is that white girl?" Geri said, "Hey, you, white girl, what's your name?" Teri replied, "Name's Teri." Lisa added, "Hi, Stacie." Stacie said hi to Lisa. As they were leaving around the store, Mandan said, "Damn, girl, does everyone know you or what?" Stacie replied, "No, but she was in my class last year."

Untying the horses, Geri said, "Well, get on, girls, and let's ride." Mandan called, "Yeehaw! Let's move, baby, and ride like the wind!" As they rode off, Stacie waved to Lisa and Lisa waved back.

Teri asked, "You know her?" and Lisa replied, "Yeah, she was in my class last year. Her name is Stacie." "And who are the other two?" asked Teri. Lisa replied, "Not sure, but they hang around with a few others." "Who do the horses belong to?" asked Teri. "Don't know," answered Lisa. "I think they belong to that girl riding by herself." "She seems mean," noted Teri, but Lisa said, "she's OK."

While they were sitting in front of the store, a car pulled up and Jon got out. He ran into the store not noticing the girls. "You know him?" asked Teri. Lisa answered, "He's just a friend from school." Soon Jon walked out from the store holding two plastic bags of groceries. He noticed Lisa and Teri sitting out front of the store. He mostly turned his attention on Teri because she was white. He said hi, and they both said hi back. Then he got in the backseat of the car, and it drove off. As the car went eastward toward the highway, Jon kept his eyes on Teri until he could see her no more. Teri didn't notice.

A news bulletin came on TV and radio: "The clothes of the missing boy were found today in a hideout in the mountains just west of the community, according to the FBI. A memorial will be held tomorrow at the Boys & Girls Club for the missing little boy named Chuck Anderson, known as Chucky."

Sitting on the couch, watching TV, and being bored, Francis saw the news. He jumped up and grabbed his cell phone and ran toward the park. His cell phone rang as he ran, and he answered.

"Hey, Julia, what's up?" Julia asked if he'd heard the news. "Yeah, I was gonna call Tim and the rest of the gang."

Julia replied, "OK, I'll call the girls. Where you guys gonna be at?" Francis told her, "I'm going to the park. I'll call the guys and tell them to meet me there. I'll see you there and—" Julia interrupted, "Me and Meredith are in Rio. We'll be back in an hour, but the rest of the girls will meet you there. Good-bye." Francis said, "See ya," and then walked on to the park.

They all met at the park. Francis told everyone what he'd heard on the news. Geri asked, "Did they find that little boy?" "No," Francis answered, "but they found his clothes and something neat." Geri asked, "What is it?" "You guys wanna go see?" asked Francis. Tim answered, "Yeah, let's go! Are you gonna go, Stacie? It's OK if you don't." Stacie replied, "I'll go," and they all ran up to the hideout.

When they got there, they found the place all messed up and the hideout torn down. Francis said, "It looks as if they were here already and found what they were looking for." "Who?" asked Geri. Tim answered, "The police, dumb ass." Stacie asked, "What's all the little white stuff? It looks like hard milk drops." Mandan answered, "It's cement," but Geri added, "No, it's plaster." "What are they doing with plaster up here?" asked Francis.

Tim said, "Hey, look. It looks like it was made to make those oval shapes on the ground." Geri and Stacie followed the oval shapes. There were six of them. They both stopped after the last oval shape and looked at the others in fear, realizing that the shapes were of Big Foot prints. They both ran toward the others, and Geri told them what they had realized. "Yeah, right," said Tim, "What are you saying? Big Foot strikes again?" Stacie answered, "Damn straight!" "OK, we'll go have a look," said Francis.

They all saw the tracks. The strides were about five feet apart, and the prints sank in the ground about three inches. Tim asked, "Why didn't we see this before?" "'Cause we weren't looking beyond the hideout, dumb ass," answered Geri. Before anyone could say anything more, Geri was running down the mountain, and Stacie was not far behind her. Then Mandan decided to go, leaving behind Tim and Francis.

"I wonder, where the hell are the twins?" asked Tim. "They were riding on their four-wheeler and dirt bike somewhere," answered Francis. "They're probably chasing the girls," said Tim. He and Francis started back down the mountain, wondering if Big Foot did exist.

"Maybe it was Big Foot who killed Patrick," said Tim.

"Probably the police already thought of that," replied Francis.

Stacie went home, while Mandan and Geri went to Geri's. The two girls got on a horse and rode toward Tim and Francis. Tim asked, "Where you guys going?" "To the police station," answered Mandan. "Geri's mom said there's a lot of people gathered over there. We're going to see what's all the hype."

Tim and Francis walked to the police station and went inside. "What's all the excitement about?" asked Tim. "We got a molding of big feet," answered Officer Vein. "The footprints were found near a hideout up in the mountains where the little boy's clothes were found."

Tim asked, "How did you find out about a hideout?" "Someone left us a tip," answered Vern. "It was the voice of a female." "A female, huh?" asked Tim. "Hey, Francis, how many females do we know that knew about the place?" Francis asked, "You don't think it's . . . ," and Tim answered, "It could be any of them." "Geri's outside," Francis said. "Come on."

The two girls were sitting on a horse in a crowd of people. "Hey, you lesbos," Tim greeted them, "which one of you called about the hideout without telling any of us?" "Who you calling a lesbo?" asked Geri. "And we didn't call anyone. Did you?" Mandan answered, "No.

I just heard the information myself." "What did you guys see inside?" asked Geri.

"The moldings of big feet," answered Francis. "The police said they belong to Big Foot and that he probably stole that little boy. Or it's a sick game someone is playing." "Do you think he killed Patrick also?" asked Geri. "He could have," answered Francis, "but I doubt it."

Just then a Hummer arrived, and Julia and Meredith got out. They walked up to Geri and Mandan, who were still sitting on the horse. "What happened?" asked Julia. "Why is there a lot of people here?" "Did something else happen to someone?" asked Meredith. "No," answered Mandan, "the police found Big Foot prints near the hideout, and they found the little boy's clothes."

Geri asked, "Did either one of you tell the police by making an anonymous phone call?" "Me?" asked Meredith. "No way. Don't be stupid. Did you?" "Hell no," answered Julia, "I got better things to do with my time than call the police."

Everyone heard the high-pitched noise of a motor approaching. "What's that?" asked Julia. "It's Mark or Kyle," answered Mandan. Then Mark rode up on his four-wheeler, and Kyle rode up on his dirt bike with Stacie sitting behind. Mandan jumped off the horse and got on the four-wheeler behind Mark, saying, "Take me for a ride!" "Wait, I have something to say," said Mark. "We heard on the news about the little boy, and we heard about Big Foot from my uncle. Is that why everybody is here?" "Yeah," answered Francis, adding, "Where were you guys?" "We went riding around," said Kyle, "mostly at the red sand dunes."

"Are you going to ride with Mark then?" asked Geri. "Yeah," replied Mandan, "I'll meet you at Stacie's house in a little while." "I'll race you guys to the red sand dunes and back," said Geri. "You're on!" answered Mark. "Hey, babe, you better hang on!" "Don't worry about me," said Mandan.

Off from the police station they went. Between Mr. Meens's store and Geri's house and stables, they rode in a cloud of dust, having fun like there was no tomorrow. Across the open range of dirt, rocks, and thorny bushes, the horse galloped with Geri tucked down to cut through the wind. Mark rode full throttle with Mandan on the back, holding onto Mark and her hair blowing around in the wind. "God, it must be good to be young," remarked Mr. Meens. "Look at them ride."

The red sand dunes was a place south of the community of Grey Stalk, about two miles away. It was on the reservation and was a place where most of the children went to have fun. Anyone who wanted to go on a wild ride could because there were no laws there for any kind of vehicles. There were no roads to it, and the terrain was really rough.

At the police station, someone said, "You police should go out and stop those kids from riding like that." She was concerned. Vern answered, "We can't, ma'am. Those kids are not on a public road and are free to go out there if they want. That is the law around here."

The three were at the red sand dunes by then, and they stayed awhile. As Kyle and Stacie were riding out, they saw a wolf. It was a black one, and it darted out at them from nowhere. Stacie screamed and wrapped her legs around Kyle's waist. "Look at that dog!" she yelled. Kyle said, "I don't think it's a dog!" "What is it," asked Stacie, "a coyote?" "It's too big," answered Kyle. "It looks like a wolf." But then he thought there were not supposed to be wolves around. "Go faster," screamed Stacie. "Go faster!"

In a panic and fearful of being bitten, she screamed. The wolf ran after them but tired out and stopped. Kyle said, "I wonder, where the hell did that wolf come from?"

He and Stacie rode to Geri, who was walking her horse at the bottom of the dunes. "Where's Mark?" asked Kyle. "They went riding the dunes somewhere," answered Geri. "Let's go ride the dunes, too," said Stacie. Kyle told her, "Can't. This motorcycle sucks in the sand. Hey, guess what?" he asked Geri. "We saw a wolf when we were riding this way!"

"Bullshit," Geri said humorously. "No, it's true," cried Stacie. Just then Mark and Mandan flew down from the top of the dune to the ground not far from the other three, then drove over to them. "That was fun!" said Mandan. "Take me for a ride on the dunes," asked Stacie. Mark said, "Let's go," and Mandan jumped off so Stacie could climb on. "You better hang on, girl," warned Mandan.

As the four-wheeler sped off, Kyle told Mandan about the wolf they had seen. Mandan said, "I'm riding back with you, Geri. I'm not getting bit by no damn wolf!"

"We'll go back when Mark gets here," said Geri. "Will your horse make it back?" asked Kyle. Geri replied, "Yeah, he's pretty well rested." "He'd better be," said Mandan. "I don't want to be eaten by no wolf!"

Mark and Stacie came back laughing from riding the dunes. "Shall we head back before it gets dark?" asked Gerri. Kyle told Mark, "Hey, dude, we saw a wolf when we rode in." "What the hell is a wolf doing out here?" asked Mark. "And where did it come from?" "Don't mow," answered Kyle, and Stacie added, "I think we should all head back together." "That's cool," said Mark. "Are we riding back the way we are?" "I like where I'm at," replied Stacie. Everyone agreed to the situation, and Mark said, "Let's go!"

On the way back, they all saw the wolf. It was at a distance, sitting and watching the kids ride by. "It's freaky," said Mandan. "Ooh, I hate wolves." "Me too," added Geri. "It better not bother my horse, or my dad will shoot it. I have a rifle in my saddle, but I'm not sure how to use it."

Stacie put her head down and covered her eyes in fear. Mark and Kyle kept a close eye on the wolf. Mark was making sure it didn't try anything, thinking, *All I have for protection is a buck knife.*

Chapter Five

A New Discovery

Back in town, it wasn't long before people started leaving the police station. Francis, Julia, and the rest of the bunch headed for their homes as well. For the people of Grey Stalk, this is not normal.

Mark, Kyle, Geri, Mandan, and Stacie all rode back into town to find no one at the police station. Mark took Stacie home, and Geri took Mandan home, then left for hers. The twins rode off to their home. As night fell upon the town, everyone turned in. It was a night like no other. Main Street was empty of kids. A few cars passed up and down, but the town of Grey Stalk felt like a graveyard or a ghost town.

There was a full moon, so it was possible to see without any kind of light. Francis sat at his window, staring out. He thought, *Where is everyone tonight?* Down the street from his house, he heard a car. It drove up to Jon's house, and he saw Jon get off with his parents. "I wonder where he went," he thought. Suddenly the cell phone rang, and Francis jumped. *Damn, that scared me*, he thought.

"Hello?" Francis said. He heard Julia say, "Just calling to see what you are doing."

"Nothing," Francis answered. "I was looking out my window. There's no one around." "Kinda spooky, huh?" asked Julia. "Maybe everyone is afraid of Big Foot." "This place is getting a little crazy," replied Francis. Julia added, "I'll say. Geri called me earlier and said she went riding to the red dunes and they all saw a wolf. I wonder where the wolf came from." Francis remarked, "I wonder why it's here. Hold on, my home phone is ringing. Hello? Yeah, Julia just told me about it. She said Geri told her. Let me call you back. I'm on my cell talking to Julia. Laters. Hey, you still there?"

"Yeah," replied Julia, "who was that?" "It was Kyle," answered Francis. "He was telling me about the wolf you told me about. I'm gonna see what he wants." "OK," said Julia, "call me later." Both at the same time said bye. Francis called out, "Mom, I'm not going to Mark and Kyle's house. I'll be right back." "OK, but don't stay out late," answered his mother as he went out the front door.

Just as Francis stepped off his porch, he heard the howl of a wolf. It sounded like it was coming from the direction where the red dunes were. Then came the sound of trees crashing and rocks clashing together. Francis got scared but tried to show no fear as he walked to the twins' house. He called on his cell to tell the twins he was coming. Then he ran on the sidewalk as fast as he could. As he got closer, he heard a horse running behind him. It came closer and closer. When he got to the house, it stopped. He stood at the front door, breathing heavily. He made a phone call. Geri's cell phone rang. "Hello, big boy," she answered, "looking for a good time?" "Hey," replied Francis, "I think one of your horses got out. I heard it down the street." "Which one?" asked Geri. Francis replied, "I don't know. It's dark outside." "Thanks," said Geri. "I'll tell my dad. What are you doin'? And why ya breathing so hard? It turns me on." "Really?" asked Francis. "Just kidding," she replied. "Bye."

Francis heard a lot of noise coming from inside the house. He knocked, and someone said, "Come in." He went in to find Jon with the twins playing Xbox on TV. "Whatcha all playing?" he asked. "Mortal Combat Six," replied Mark, and Francis replied, "Cool!" Kyle asked him, "Why you breathing so hard? Did you run over here?" Francis answered, "Yeah, I thought I heard a wolf howling from the red dunes, and then I heard something in the woods. It sounded like it was knocking down trees and smashing rocks together." Jon cried, "Oh shit!"

The cell phone rang, and Francis answered, "What's up?" "My dad said all the horses are still in the stables," Geri told him. "I wonder what that was following me," said Francis, "'cause it sounded like one of your horses. I thought you were out riding tonight. Unless it's a wild one." "Wild horses aren't usually alone," said Geri. "They stay in herds. And I don't think they would follow anyone." "Hmm, freaky!" replied Francis. Geri added, "Hopefully, it was nothing. What are you doin'?" "Just hanging out at the twins' house," said Francis. "The nasty boys? Who's all there?" asked Geri. Francis answered, "All of us except Tim. Don't know where he is. Maybe he's at home? And you?" "I'm at home," said Geri. "Mandan's at Stacie's. Not sure of Julia and Meredith." "I know Julia's at home," replied Francis. "She called earlier. I'll talk to you tomorrow."

"Good-bye."

Francis turned to Mark. "Hey, Mark, go get Tim on your four-wheeler."

"See if he's home, first," replied Mark. Francis made the call. While he talked on his cell, Jon and the twins went outside. Out the corner of Jon's eye in a blur, Jon saw a man standing at the corner of the house. He was just outside of the light that was shining from the porch light, but then he was gone.

"You guys see that?" asked Jon. "See what?" said Kyle, and Mark said, "I saw nothing." Kyle added, "What did you see?" "I thought I saw a man standing by the corner of the house," said Jon, and the boys darted around the corner of the house, but they saw nothing. Since they didn't look on the ground for tracks, they didn't see the hoof marks in the dirt. The boys heard barking from a distance at somebody's house. "I bet that's him," said Jon.

Francis got off his cell. The whole time he'd sat and listened to Tim's mom talking about being good and listening to your parents and being a good example for other kids and so on, before she said Tim could go over to the twins' and visit. "My God, the lady can talk," remarked Francis as he went outside. "All she had to say was yes or no. Damn!" Finding no one, he said, "Hey, where did everyone go? Where you guys at?"

Jon and the twins were in back of the house, listening to the dogs barking from other peoples' homes. They heard Francis yelling for them, and Jon yelled, "We're back here!" "What are you doing back there?" asked Francis. Mark answered, "Jon thought he saw a guy standing at the corner of our house. If it was a guy, he sure runs fast, 'cause he was gone before Kyle or me saw anything." "You sure it wasn't your daddy?" asked Francis. "To hell with you," said Jon, "it wasn't."

"Oh, Tim's mom said he can come over," said Francis. "Are you going to get him?" The boys walked back into the house. "Yeah," replied Mark, "let me get my keys."

Mark went back outside and was about to start his four-wheeler when he heard a howl, a long, low howl from a distance. He thought, *I bet it's that wolf we saw earlier today.* Trying not to think about it and showing no fear, he started the four-wheeler and drove off.

Riding down the street, Mark saw no cars and nobody out and about. He said to himself, *This is freaky as hell.* He rode up to Tim's house and left the four-wheeler running as he got off. He ran to the front door and knocked. Tim opened the door with a surprised look on his face. "Well, don't just stand there," Mark said. "Let's go!" Tim replied, "Go where?" "To my house, stupid. Didn't Francis call you?" asked Mark, then added, "Can I use your phone?" "Yeah," said Tim.

Mark called Francis and asked, "Didn't you ask Tim?" But Francis informed him that he spoke to his mother, not Tim. Mark replied, "Shit, you should have told me that," and hung up the phone. To Tim he said, "Francis called your mom earlier and asked if you could come over. She said yes. Do you want to?" "Yeah," answered Tim, "let's go. Are we going to walk or run to your house?" Mark answered, "We're going to ride. Get on!" "Cool," said Tim, adding, "Wait. Let me grab some games and some CDs." Then they both got on and drove into the moonlit night.

They got to Mark's house and started to go inside when they heard a noise in the woods. It was the same noise Francis heard on his way over to the twins' house. "Listen!" said Mark. "I wonder what it is." Tim went inside and called everyone outside to hear the noise.

Tim, who lived by logic, thought of something else besides Big Foot. "Maybe it's cattle moving about in the woods."

"Maybe it's Big Foot!" said Mark. "Maybe it's Jon's daddy," said Francis, laughing. Jon replied, "Maybe it's your mommy!" and laughed. Tim said, "Whatever it is, it sounds like it's staying up in the woods."

Stacie, who lived close to the woods, could hear the noise and called the police and the Game and Fish Conservation officers, then told her dad. Her dad fired a few gunshots into the woods, which set off a series of phone calls through the community. The police station was flooded with phone calls, people wanting more information on the gunshots heard. Mrs. Anderson thought someone got shot and was asking who it was. The police replied that no one had been shot and asked everyone to stay in their homes. The police heard from the callers that the shots came from Stacie's house and rushed over. They were at Stacie's house for half an hour or so.

Francis's cell phone rang. "Hey, Julia, what's up?" "What's going on at Stacie's house?" asked Julia. "Not sure," replied Francis. "It might have to do with gunfire from her house." "Is everyone all right? Do you know?" asked Julia. Francis said, "Why don't you call her and find out?" Julia replied, "OK, I'll call you right back."

The phone rang at Stacie's house. "Hello," she answered. Julia asked, "Hey, what happened? Is everyone all right?" "Yeah," Stacie said. "We heard some scary noises in the woods, and my dad fired his gun into the woods." "What kinda noise?" asked Julia. "Loud, crushing noise of trees falling and rocks or something rolling down the hill." "Did you call the police?" asked Julia. "Yeah," replied Stacie. "They sent some police up into the mountains with guns." "Francis said he and the guys heard gunshots from your house," explained Julia. "I saw the police at your house and called Francis. Well, if everything is OK, I'll call you later."

"Bye."

There was more gunfire up in the mountains. One of the policemen yelled, "Help me! I'm being attacked!" He kept yelling, and the animals growled. It growled the way bears do when they attack. The police force got to where the man was yelling, but nothing was there.

Just blood stains, bullet shells, and Big Foot prints and boot tracks everywhere.

Law enforcement spent the rest of the night looking for the missing policeman but found nothing. They brought in dogs for the search, but they were too scared to go up in the mountains.

The police force did not know what to do or how to handle the situation. They had a dead, torn-up teenage boy and a missing little boy and a fallen police officer. That also stirred up concerns in the community of Grey Stalk. As the search continued throughout the night, the police called in the FBI and search-and-rescue squads.

It was just before dawn when two more men were found dead, one a policeman and one from the FBI. The policeman had a broken neck and a broken back, a hole in his skull and in his stomach, and bruises all over. The FBI agent was ripped into pieces, with body parts lying around and some body parts missing, too, like Patrick Larson, except the scene with the agent was worse.

This kept the entire community on edge. They could hear radio transmissions from the police cars, and informed one another by phone of the situation in the mountains. It was a long and scary night for everyone.

It was a long week after that, with no incidents and two funerals. The community was in shock and shaken up pretty badly. But life goes on as it usually does in Grey Stalk. The police department paid for one funeral, and the FBI paid for the other. The police had their hands full and tied with these murders.

There was soon a news bulletin for the attention of the people of Grey Stalk: "Since the recent murders that took place, we urge everyone to be indoors at dusk. No one is to be out after dark. It is not a law but a precaution. Thank you for your support and participation. The Grey Stalk Police Department."

The police held a memorial for the missing police officer. Everyone from Grey Stalk was there, including the ten kids who were all friends. Tim said, "I hate funerals. They're sad and everyone cries, and it makes me feel somehow." Julie told him, "This is a memorial, not a funeral, stupid." Tim, in a sassy way, said, "Shut up. I guess we'll never go camping again." Francis replied, "We will as soon as they kill that son of a b—" but Julia interrupted, "You don't have to say it like that." When the memorial was over, everyone went home. Another week passed, and everything was getting back to normal. People still talked about what happened, but they let the police and the FBI deal with it.

One afternoon, Francis decided to go buy a Coke. It was just after 2 p.m., and the store closed at 6 p.m. He ran down the street, thinking, *Man, it's hot today. Can't wait for that ice-cold cup of icy pop.* He ran by the park and saw Jon playing in the park with Stacie. Francis said, "Hi, you two. I'm going to the store. Want anything?" They answered, "Gimme a Coke." Francis said, "You got it," and took off running.

He got to the store and pushed the door to go in, but slammed into it instead. "What the," he said. The sign on the door said Closed. *I guess Mr. Meens must be sick today,* he said to himself. He stood there and thought, *Hmm, I wonder how far it is to the convenience store? I can make it. OK, legs, haul ass.*

Back at the park, after a few hours had passed, Stacie said, "I'm real thirsty." Jon said, "Me too. I wonder where's Francis. It don't take that long to walk to the store."

Francis ran down Main Street, panting and sweating. He said, "Man, I didn't think it would take this long!" Then a car pulled up. It was Geri and her mom, and Geri's head was sticking out the passenger window. "Hey, big boy, want a ride?" she asked. Francis, panting and sweating, said, "Sure," and got in.

Geri's mom asked, "Where you going in such a hurry?" He answered, "The convenience store. If you can drop me off there, I can walk back." They pulled up to the convenience store and stopped. "Thank you," Francis said as he got off. Francis bought the Cokes and had just started back when Officer Sicord pulled up in his patrol car. "Hey, son," he said, "you want a ride? I can give you a ride to the police station." "Cool," said Francis as he jumped in. Officer Sicord asked what he was doing all the way out there, and Francis answered, "Mr. Meens's store was closed today, so I ran down to the convenience store." Officer Sicord looked at Francis and said, "Yes, I know.

He had a heart attack yesterday. I guess he was just old and done too much work in the store."

Francis could not believe it. "Are you sure he's not sick or something?" he asked. "Who found him?" Sicord said, "He was found dead in his store by the old lady named Olga." Francis said, "She probably killed him by her looks," and laughed, trying to show no emotions. Sicord said, "Did you say something?" "No," Francis replied.

Sicord told him, "Here we are." Francis thanked him and got out of the police car. He called Tim to tell him about Mr. Meens; then calls went to the rest of the bunch except Jon, who was still at the park. Francis started walking toward the park.

The sun had just set behind the mountains, and Jon decided to go home. He had played long enough and had forgotten about Francis bringing him a Coke. He thought about what the police had said about no one being out after dark and to never be alone. Stacie had left when the sun was just above the mountains. She was too thirsty to play any longer, so had left Jon alone.

He was on his way home when he ran into a little man. The little man seemed to have popped out of nowhere, and Jon was deep in thought about getting home. The little man said, "Hi, fella! Where you going?" "Home," said Jon in a scared, shaky voice. The little man scared Jon by the way he looked.

The little man said, "I know of a place where there is lots of toys and candy." Jon said, "Where?" The little man replied, "Come with me, and I'll show you." "No," Jon said, "I have to get home, or my mom will be pissed off at me." The little man grabbed Jon's arm and said, "You are not going anywhere! You are going with me!"

Jon saw he was bigger than the little man and pulled his arm away, saying, "To hell with you, you little shit!" He pushed the little man. Just as Jon was going to hit the little man, he felt a sharp pain in his back where another little man stabbed him with his knife. Blood started to come out, and Jon let out a scream of pain as he tried to put his hand on his back. Then more little men appeared. They came out from the playground equipment. Jon felt another sharp pain in his lower leg, from a spear, and he dropped to his knees, holding the cut on his leg. The little men, who hid everywhere, were coming out after Jon, stabbing and cutting him up. They were trying to butcher him. Jon cried for help just as a rope was put around his neck. He cried, "Someone help me!" as he was pulled to the ground.

A little man jumped on Jon's chest with a knife and then disappeared. The little man went flying off Jon. There was Francis, kicking and fighting the little men, yelling, "You leave my friend alone!" Francis took out his buck knife and started stabbing little men everywhere, blood flying this way and that way! Then Francis felt a pain in the back of his thigh where a knife cut him. As blood started coming from Francis, he said, "Now I'm pissed off!"

While trying to help Jon and fighting for his life, Francis did not give up. He killed three of the little men in the fight and wounded several others. The little men gave up fighting. They ran off, carrying their dead away. Francis did not notice which way they went because he turned his attention to Jon.

Jon was lying in a pool of blood, barely conscious. He said to Francis, "I don't wanna die. I don't wanna die!" Francis told him, "Don't worry. I'm gonna get help." Jon cried, "Don't leave me, please!" and he lost consciousness. Francis called 911 from his cell.

The police arrived in no time. Francis also called Jon's parents and then called the whole gang. The police wanted a statement from Francis, but by then, he and Jon were already being put into the ambulance. Everyone showed up at the park, except for Jon's and Francis's parents because the boys were being airlifted to the hospital in Rio. Julia called Francis on his cell and said she was going to the hospital and would give a ride to whoever wanted to come. Francis said, "OK, I'll meet you there." Julia asked, "How's Jon?" Francis responded, "He's unconscious and won't stop bleeding. But the paramedics are tending to him." Francis had a lump in his throat and was about to cry, but he held it all in. He said, "We're getting on the helicopter now. I'll see y'all at the hospital." Then they flew off.

Chapter Six

What Happens Next

While Francis and Jon and their parents all flew to the hospital, the police started an immediate investigation. The FBI came also, to cover more ground. They told everyone to leave, and they taped off the playground with yellow tape. Officers Sicord and Vern were told to go to the hospital and get a statement from the kids. The other kids left one by one with their parents. They were given a police escort to the hospital.

Tim and the twins were concerned but did not show it. The girls were all scared and were comforted by their mothers. Mandan grabbed Stacie and held her in a hugging position. Geri was comforted by her big sister Tiffany, who could be crazy at times and made people laugh, but at this time was being supportive and understanding for Geri. Tiffany told Geri to think positive thoughts for Jon.

Julia and Meredith were worried about Jon. They all rushed to the hospital as if Jon was their own little brother. Tim wondered what had happened. He thought to himself, *If anybody beat up on Jon, I swear I'm gonna kick their ass.*

Back at the playground, police were taking pictures of the area. The pictures showed little footprints, little tools and ropes. The police took moldings of the little footprints, gathered up all the tools and ripped-up clothing and Francis's buck knife. The FBI took blood samples and sent them to the forensic lab for studying. They also sent dogs out to follow the little footprints on the ground.

Lisa was standing by her friend Teri at the playground. Teri said, "Here we go again," as the police asked questions. They asked about what had happened and did anyone see anything. Everyone they asked said no.

The rescue helicopter landed at the hospital. The hospital emergency unit was waiting to take Jon to surgery. Another nurse tended to Francis's cuts and bruises while the surgeons worked on Jon in OR.

The police arrived at the hospital. After Francis was stitched up, the doctor said he could go home. The police asked Francis's parents if they could talk to him first. Francis said he would be willing to tell the police whatever they wanted to know. The police started questioning him.

Soon the rest of the gang came in. Stacie was the first to ask how Jon was. Jon's mother responded, "He just went into surgery, and the doctor said nothing to us." All the girls stayed by Jon's mom. The boys went to Francis to hear what had happened. Francis said, "First Mr. Meens, and now Jon." Then they all went to the waiting room. They all comforted each other and fell asleep there. Everyone stayed at the hospital through the night.

As night passed, the police and FBI were on the trail of the little men who'd attacked Jon and Francis. They followed the footprints to a cave. The cave had a narrow opening. The dogs went in first, barking and sniffing about, and the police followed. They came to a big open space deep in the cave. The whole cave was made of rock, and the floor was solid rock with a fire pit in the middle, where a fire was burning.

The large space in the cave was big enough to fit at least fifty people. On the walls were drawings of long ago. The police looked at all the drawings and took pictures. They saw a drawing of a little man attacking a young Indian girl and then of little women cutting her up, then of the whole village eating. There were many drawings like that. There were also many smaller caves that went in different directions.

On the floor of the cave, they found hides, human and animal skulls, bones, and little tools like axes, ropes, and spears, as well as kitchen utensils like forks, pots, pans, bowls, and so on. An FBI agent said, "These little people must have stolen all this stuff."

After carefully examining everything, including the drawings on the cave walls, another agent said, "I'll bet these little men are the ones that killed Patrick Larson." "And stole the little boy," the first agent said. "I disagree with you, because if you look at all the drawings on the wall of the cave, you'll see they're all the same. That is, they attack and kill the victims, bag them, then take it home. I think Patrick was too big, and they left him there but took what parts they could carry. That's why Jon was attacked, because he's small. The little men attack on the spot wherever they're at, if they have to. Chucky was carried off somewhere. With Chucky, there was no sign of a fight, struggle, or blood stains anywhere. But now we know where these little people live, we'll keep an eye out for them."

The other agent said, "Now we have to find Chucky, if he's still alive." The first agent said, "We still have to find these little people as well." They radioed in some more agents, and the two went back to make a report. The first agent said, "It's been a long night. It'll be daylight soon. I wonder how that boy is doing at the hospital. I think his name was Jon."

Back at the hospital, it was now daylight, and the surgeon came to see the family in the waiting room. He said, "I need to see the parents of the little boy named Jon." Jon's mother and father stepped up to the doctor in fear of the news. The mother asked, "How's Jon? How's my baby?" The doctor said, "He has too much extensive damage done to the body. We did as much as we could. We put him in ICU for now. We'll have to wait and see. If we have to, we'll open him up again, but for now we'll see if he can heal." Jon's parents asked if they could see him now. The kids had woken up in time to hear the news and asked if they could see him also. The doctor responded, "Only two at a time. Jon's parents go in first."

Jon's parents saw Jon lying there, wrapped in bandages and in stitches. Jon's mother cried, asking, "Why? Why my little boy? He's done nothing wrong to no one." She was comforted by her husband as they held Jon's hands.

They let the kids in by pairs. The first two were Francis and Tim, then Mandan and Stacie, then Julia and Meredith. Next, the twins went in, then Geri and her older sister Tiffany. Even though they were all his friends, Stacie took it hardest. The kids were told to go home and that they would be notified if anything should come up.

A new bulletin went out to the people of Grey Stalk Community: "There have been some strange happenings in our community. Take precautions. Children, do not wander out at night by yourselves. If you see anything out of the ordinary, call your local police or FBI. Thank you."

One day, everyone was out and about as if nothing had happened. The twins, Mark and Kyle, went on a ride with Mandan and Stacie. Julia and Meredith went back into the town of Rio to go shopping. Tim and Francis stayed at Tim's house playing video games. They all had Jon on their minds but still tried to go about their business and have a positive outlook for him. The twins took Mandan and Stacie to the red sand dunes. Tiffany and Geri went horseback riding behind the schools.

The police got the results from the lab, saying there were three different types of blood at the crime scene. They belonged to Jon and Francis, and tests showed that the third blood type was from an unknown species.

At the hospital, Jon was still lying in his bed unconscious, hooked up to four different kinds of IVs and covered with bloodstained bandages. His mother and father were at his side. Jon's mother answered a knock on the door, and Lisa came in. It looked like she had already been crying. Lisa said, "I just heard the news today." Between sniffles, she asked if Jon was going to be all right. "Jon is my friend," she said. "He was always nice to me in school. I wish I could do something for him." She held his hand for a few minutes and then left the room. She told Teri, who was waiting outside the room, "I wish I could do something for him." Teri said, "Maybe you can, when the time is right. Let's go to my house." So they left the hospital.

Out at the red sand dunes, the twins were riding with Mandan and Stacie. Mark said, "It's funny, but I don't see that wolf out here." Mandan said, "I don't want to see that wolf anywhere." They all rode to Mandan's house. They heard her parents fighting, so they went to Stacie's house instead.

Stacie went inside when the phone rang, and answered it, "Hello, who is this?" "This is Julia. I'm with Meredith. We're in Rio, and we're going to see Jon. Are you going?" Stacie responded, "Yes, I guess I can take whomever with me." Julia asked, "Who's all with you?" and Stacie replied, "Mandan and the twins." "Oh God, why you with the twins?" asked Julia. "Those perverts!" Stacie replied, "I know, but they take us anywhere we want to go." Julia said, "OK, we'll meet you guys there."

"Bye."

Francis and Tim were still playing video games when Francis's cell phone rang. He answered to hear Julia on the other end. "Hey, babe, what's up?" he asked. Julia said, "Are you going to see Jon anytime today?" Francis responded, "Yeah, Tim's going to take me. I'm at his house. Where are you at?" Julia said, "I'm in Rio with Meredith. We'll be at the hospital later." Francis finished, "OK," and hung up.

At 6 p.m., everyone started to show up at the hospital, little by little. Julia and Meredith were first to arrive. The twins showed up with Mandan and Stacie. A few minutes later, Francis and Tim showed up. Francis was still mad about what the little men had done to Jon, but he was also freaked out about them. He hadn't talked about them to anybody, and he wasn't sure he wanted to.

Julia and Meredith came out of the ICU and said, "Whoever wants to can go in." So Mandan and Stacie went in. Julia asked, "Where's Geri? Anyone seen her? I tried to call her house, but no answer." Francis replied, "Maybe she went riding on her horse." Meredith commented, "She sure loves that horse."

Mandan and Stacie came out, Stacie with her head on Mandan's shoulder, saying, "I hate whoever did this to him." Meredith asked, "Does anyone know what happened or seen what happened to Jon?" Francis said, "I do, but I'll tell you when I come back out from seeing him." He and Tim went into Jon's room. When they came out, Francis told his friends to sit while he told them what had happened.

Meanwhile, Geri and her sister Tiffany were out horseback riding. The sun was setting on the mountain top. They had ridden from the school out to the sand dunes. Then Geri said to Tiffany, "Sister, we better get home. I wanna go see Jon at the hospital." So they started back home. Geri said with excitement, "Hey, I'll race you home!" and Tiffany said, "You're on!"

They were racing side by side when all of a sudden Geri's horse fell to the ground, trapping one of Geri's legs underneath. Tiffany, who was going full speed, slowed her horse down. "Whoa!" she said as she turned the horse around. She saw a man standing over Geri. Geri was screaming in pain and in fear of the tall man. Since it was almost dark, she could not see all the features of his body. He was saying, "This is my land, and I don't want you or anyone on it!" While crying in pain, Geri said, "Go to hell!"

Tiffany arrived and said, "Yeah, eat shit and die! You leave my little sister alone." Just then, the tall man kicked Geri's horse and busted its head wide open, killing it while the horse was still on the ground. Then he grabbed Geri and said, "I will kill you as an example to others." Then he hit Geri, though Geri was trying to fight him off. Tiffany made her horse kick him. The horse kicked him in the stomach. The tall man was winded and fell to the ground. Tiffany got off, reached for a small flashlight that was in the saddle bag of her horse, and shined it on Geri. "Are you OK, Sister?" she asked.

Tiffany then shined the light on the tall man. He had just stood up from his knees. Tiffany, shining the light up and down the man, saw his hairy legs and cloven hooves instead of feet. She grabbed Geri while looking at the man, and said, "What the hell are you? Are you a goat or something?" Remembering the saddles were always well supplied, she reached over to Geri's saddle on the dead horse and grabbed the .30-30 rifle.

The tall man kicked Geri in the head, and she fell over. Tiffany fired two shots at him. The first shot, she missed him, and the second shot blew a hole in his chest. He ran off into the darkness, staggering.

Tiffany, in a panic, put Geri on her horse and then got on, and they rode top speed home.

When they got home, Tiffany called 911. The police arrived within a minute or two. Tiffany said, "I didn't know Geri was hurt this bad!" Their parents asked, "What happened?" Tiffany described the situation to their parents as the paramedics were on their way, saying, "It's kinda weird, but here goes." She explained her story about the Goat Man. Her dad asked, "Have you been drinking?" and Tiffany answered, "No! I'm telling you the truth. If Geri was awake, she'd tell you the same thing."

The ambulance arrived at Tiffany's house, and their dad left in his truck. Tiffany and her mom got in the ambulance and rode with Geri to the helipad behind the casino, to be airlifted to the hospital in Rio.

Meanwhile, Geri's dad went out riding to the school area. Using the spotlight, he found nothing. On his way back, he was greeted by the Fish and Game Conservation officers. One of the COs asked, "Can we help you, Mister?" Geri's dad said, "Yeah, I'm looking for a Goat Man." "A Goat Man?" asked the guys from Fish and Game. "Are you crazy? I guess we can help you look for him." Then, out to the sand dunes they drove. The men from Fish and Game were confused but followed Geri's dad anyway.

The father managed to find the trail his daughters had been on. He followed it to the spot where the dead horse was lying. He got off his truck to examine the horse. He saw a hole in the horse's head, right between the eyes, and said, "This does not look like a gunshot. What the hell happened here?"

There was blood here and there, boot tracks, horse tracks, and cloven hoof tracks. The COS said, "Holy shit! What animal made this?" A police officer arrived on a four-wheeler to see if anything had been found. They all started talking about what they saw.

Meanwhile, from the helicopter to another ambulance, the patient was taken to the hospital. Tim saw the ambulance arrive and said, "Cool! Hey, guys, the ambulance just came in. I wonder if it's a car crash or something." As they all looked on with Tim, they saw a body, but it was covered, and there were IVs hooked up to the patient. Then they saw Tiffany and her mom. Julia said, "No, it better not be!"

The paramedics rushed by with Geri. Her face was covered with an oxygen mask. Tiffany and her mom rushed by with doctors, nurses, and Geri in a gurney. Shortly thereafter, some teenage high schoolers came in looking for Tiffany. They were friends, all girls.

Tiffany was about five foot ten, with an hourglass-shaped body and nice facial complexion that made her very popular in school. Her little sister was not far behind her as becoming a real looker for guys. Tiffany was in high school, but she looked like she could be in college. Since she always dyed her hair, no one knew the exact color of it. Right now, it was a long, sandy-blonde color.

Now Julia and the rest of the bunch were worried. As they focused on Geri in the OR, the kids didn't hear the speaker in the ceiling. "Code blue. We have a code blue in ICU. All medical personnel available to ICU." Being so concerned for Geri, the kids failed to hear it, but five minutes later, Jon's parents came out. His mom was crying. Mandan saw and asked, "What's wrong?" "Jon's gone. My baby is gone," cried the mother. Stacie heard and fell to her knees. Mandan joined her on the floor, putting her arms around her. Julia asked, "What happened? I thought he was OK." Jon's mother said that the doctor told her the damage to Jon's organs was too extensive and that he was lucky to have lived this long.

Francis heard about Jon's death and left the hospital, thinking to himself, *Man, this really pisses me off!* Tim went after him. The twins just stayed seated with mixed feelings. Julia and Meredith joined Mandan and Stacie on the floor, all crying together.

Julia told Stacie to get up and go see Jon. Stacie got up, went into the room, and made her way to the bed Jon lay. She gave Jon a hug and said, "I love you, Jon. You were always good to me." The girls all gave Jon a hug when they came into the room. The twins then came in to see Jon. Not knowing what to say, they held his hands, then left.

Tim was having a talk with Francis. They both came back into the hospital to see Jon. Everyone was in Jon's room except the twins. The nurse told everyone to leave while they took the body and got it ready for the coroners to pick up.

The girls wanted to hear the news on Geri. All the parents waited patiently while the kids focused their attention on Geri. Scared and confused about Jon's death and Geri in surgery, the kids were exhausted. They were told to go home and wait, so everyone left.

The surgery went well. The doctors put a plastic plate in Geri's skull to cover the hole, and took a skin graft from her leg to cover the plate in her head. Tiffany's friends left when hearing the news that Geri was going to be all right.

The boys went to the twins' house. Mandan went to Stacie's house with her, and Meredith stayed at .Iulia's. The boys wanted to get their minds off Jon, so Francis said, "Let's go riding." Kyle didn't feel like riding, so he told Tim he could ride his dirt bike. Tim said, "Cool," and took off. Francis told Mark, "Go first. I'll ride after you." Tim waited at the street corner. It was dark, and Tim didn't want to ride alone. Mark finally came and said, "Where to?" Tim said, "Let's go to the convenience store." Mark replied, "OK, you first," and they both rode off.

They were both riding pretty fast. Just as they got to Mr. Meens's store, Tim saw the old lady. He saw her decayed, old, dying face, and it scared him and he wrecked. Mark rode past him before he could stop and turn around. Tim fell to the ground because a wolf jumped on him. It started biting his leg, and Tim cried out, "Mark, help me!" Mark got there and ran over the wolf. The wolf rolled, let out a cry, then ran off. In the process of running over the wolf, Mark had bounced and fell off his four-wheeler. Tim was still lying on the ground with his pants leg chewed up and his leg bleeding from bites and scratches. He was about to go into shock, but managed to get on the dirt bike and ride it back to the twins' house, while Mark rode behind him, keeping an eye out for the wolf.

They arrived at the twins' house. Francis saw Tim and said, "What the hell happened to you?" Then he saw Tim's leg and said, "Holy shit, did those little men do this to you?" Tim could hardly talk. In a panic, Mark cried, "Just call his parents!" Tim was taken to the hospital by his parents. He told his parents, "I was in a bike accident."

While he was in the hospital, he asked for Geri. He said she was his friend and he wanted to know how she was doing. The nurse said, "She's going to be all right." Then the doctor said, "Now sit still. This is going to hurt a little. I'm gonna sew you up." Tim was sewn up and brought home. He told everybody that Geri was doing fine and would be home in two days. Francis said, "That's cool. I'll call Julia and tell her." Mark had explained what had happened to Tim while he was at the hospital. Francis didn't want to sound concerned, but he was worried about what happened to Tim. He called Julia and told her about Geri. Julia said, "I know. Tiffany called and told me. How did you know about it?" Francis told her Tim had been attacked by a wolf and was taken to the hospital, and that's when he found out, from the doctor. Julia responded, "Is Tim OK?" Francis said, "Yeah, he's tough. Well, I just called to tell you that. I gotta go. Laters."

"Bye."

The next two days passed, and there were a few more killings and kidnappings. The FBI was boggled and did not know how to catch those who were doing all the killings.

Geri finally came home late in the afternoon of the second day. She made a few phone calls to tell some of the bunch that she was home. Everyone went to her house to see her. She said, "Everyone's here except Jon. Where's Junior? Is he still in the hospital?" Julia said in a calm voice, "I have something to tell you." Geri looked at all of them and at Julia. Suddenly Geri's attitude changed from being happy she was home to a look of concern, and she asked in a shaky voice, "What is it?" Julia said calmly and slowly, "Jon died. He died in the hospital the day you had your accident. Do you remember your accident?"

Geri thought, then said, "No. I remember my horse fell to the ground. My leg was trapped underneath him. I was in a lot of pain. And I remember a man standing over me. He said something, but I don't remember what. And I knew my sister was with me, and that's all. Then I woke up in the hospital with a splitting headache."

Then Geri started crying, "I can't believe he's gone. Damn it, he's just a kid. He's not supposed to die." Stacie gave her a hug and almost cried, telling her, "He was our friend also." They all sat in the living room at Geri's house and talked and laughed about the early years. Then Geri said, "When is the funeral?" "They already had it," replied Tim. Mandan said, "I know, huh? I wonder why the parents had it so quick." Geri said she felt bad because she had missed the funeral, but she couldn't help it. Everyone said they understood.

The sun was setting on the mountains and everyone said their good-byes and left. Everyone went back to their own homes except for Mandan. She went to Stacie's house and stayed the night.

The next day, late in the morning, the twins were out riding on their four-wheeler and dirt bike. Francis was practicing guitar. Mandan and Stacie were playing in front of Stacie's house. Geri was on another horse. Julia was on her porch, talking on her cell phone. Meredith and Tim were walking to the convenience store by Main Street. Mark and Kyle rode by them and stopped. Mark said, "You two are a bit of an odd couple," and Tim said, "So are you two." They all laughed.

Kyle asked, "Where you two going?" Tim pointed and said, "To the convenience store." Mark offered, "Hop on, and we'll give you all a ride." So they rode to the convenience store, bought a few things, and rode back.

Tim said, "Drop us off at the park, and go tell everyone to meet us there." Kyle asked, "Why?" Tim said, "I have something to tell everyone." The twins left and in a few minutes came back with Mandan and Stacie. Julia and Francis were walking up the road, and then Geri rode up on another horse. Francis and Julia showed up, and Francis asked, "OK, we're all here. What's up?"

Tim said, "You know that day I got into a bike accident?" Francis said, "Yeah, what about it?" Mark added, "That's when the wolf jumped on you. I still would like to kill that son of a b—" Mandan interrupted, "Let Tim talk."

Tim continued that he had seen the old lady's face. "It looked as if it was already decaying and almost a face of a skeleton. It scared me so much I thought my heart stopped, and I lost control of the dirt bike and wrecked. Then that wolf jumped on me. It came out of nowhere." Mark said, "I thought the wolf jumped out and grabbed your leg, and that's how you wrecked." Tim continued, "No, it was the sight of Olga's face that did it all." Francis said, "I wonder if the wolf belongs to her. And maybe she was the one who killed Mr. Meens." Julia said, "Oh, come on," but Francis continued, "No, I'm serious. The police told me that Mr. Meens had a heart attack. Maybe Mr. Meens saw her face, too. But because he was old, he couldn't handle it."

Just then, Lisa walked up, saying hi to Stacie. Stacie greeted her back, and Lisa said, "I want to tell y'all something scary I saw." Mandan asked, "What is it?" Lisa started, "The day you got jumped by the wolf, Tim, I was coming to see Teri. Only she didn't know I was standing behind her by the store. I was going to sneak up on her and scare her from behind. Just before I got to her, I saw her get on her hands and knees. I was wondering what she was doing. While you guys were riding toward the store, she started turning into a wolf. Then Olga came out from nowhere. She was facing the street, so she didn't see me. She yelled something, and the wolf darted out. I don't know what she said, but it didn't sound like anything I ever heard before."

Stacie said, "Teri is really a wolf? Here I wanted to be friends with her. Shit, that's messed up." Lisa said, "Yeah, I know. That sucks for me, too. I heard she had scared a few other people, and I also heard that the wolf was the one that brought home the food. The wolf eats what it can, then brings home the rest."

Meredith asked, "Why is all this happening?" Francis answered, "Don't know, but I'm sure we'll find out sooner or later." They all sat and talked about the little men, Big Foot, Olga and her daughter, and the Goat Man. It stirred up memories in everybody's mind, and Stacie said, "I miss Jon." Everyone then focused their attention on Jon. They talked until almost sunset, and then they all went home, everyone to their own house.

It was dark now and Mandan was at home by herself, ready for her evening to start as it usually did by both parents coming home drunk. First, her mom came home drunk and went straight to bed. Then Mandan's father came home, drunk also, and went straight into his bedroom. From behind their closed bedroom door, Mandan could hear her father beat her mom.

Mandan beat on her parents' bedroom door, yelling, "I'm tired of this! I'm leaving and never coming back!" She set her mind on going to Stacie's house. Mandan went out the front door screaming, "To hell with both of you! One of these days, they'll be sorry."

She grabbed her backpack and left, slamming the door. She ran down the street to Stacie's house. On her way, she ran into something big and tall. It was hairy all over, and it smelled like the hideout the kids had found on their campout. Mandan stopped, saying, "Holy shit, in fear! You're Big Foot!" She turned around and ran back to her house, but he grabbed her from behind and picked her up. She screamed and kicked, hitting him as hard as she could, but it didn't affect him in any way. She lost her backpack in the struggle.

From a distance, she could hear sirens from police cars. Mandon screamed, "Somebody help me! This hairy asshole!" But the police went to Francis's house due to his loud guitar playing. The neighbor's dogs were barking at Big Foot, but no one paid attention. Mandon passed out in fear. Big Foot put Mandan over his shoulder, and with big leaps, he was gone up into the mountains.

The next morning, Geri was riding to Mandan's house on her horse. She stopped at Mandan's, but her parents said she wasn't home and that she might be at Stacie's. Back on the horse, Geri rode down the street until she saw Mandan's backpack lying beside the road. Geri said to herself, "I wonder why that crazy girl's bag is beside the road." She picked it up and rode on to Stacie's house. She got off her horse and tied it to the old car on the side of Stacie's house, went to the front door, and knocked.

"Come in," said a voice from inside. Geri entered and asked if Mandan was there, saying, "I have her backpack." Stacie came out of the bedroom from down the hall, asking, "Did you say something?" Geri said, "Yeah, I said here's Mandan's backpack. Where's Mandan?" Stacie answered, "Well, she's not here. I haven't seen her since yesterday." So they called everybody in the gang to see if she was with any of them. No one had seen her since yesterday, they all said.

Stacie asked, "Where did you find her backpack?" Geri started for the front door, saying, "Come on, I'll show you." They both went up the street to where Mandan's backpack had been found. They both looked around to see if she was asleep in the bushes nearby. Then Geri saw big footprints on the ground, and shoe prints. Stacie said, "Those better not be Mandan's," and she started to run back to her house. "Where are you going?" called Geri. Stacie told her she was going to call the police. Geri ran back too and got on her horse. She rode back to her house and started calling everybody in the gang. She told them what she thought happened and where it had happened.

The police showed up where Stacie was standing on the side of the road in a panic. A few minutes later, Francis, Julia, and everyone showed up. Geri explained to the police and her friends what she saw and what might have happened. Francis got mad and left. Tim asked, "Where are you going?" Francis replied, "Back up to the old hideout." "I'm going with you," said Tim.

The twins parked their rides at Stacie's house and went along with Tim and Francis. The girls didn't realize the boys left until it was too late to join them. Meredith asked, "Hey, where did those guys go?" and Julia answered, "Don't know."

The boys ran all the way to the hideout and stopped there. Francis told Tim to go inside and see if anyone was there. Tim slowly went in, holding his breath, then said, "Oh shit! Hey, you guys, come here quick!" Everyone ran in to find Mandan lying on the ground. Some of her clothes were ripped off and she had no color in her face.

"I think she's dead," said Tim. Francis got mad and said, "Shut up! She's not dead!" He called Julia and told her they found Mandan. "Where?" asked Julia, and Francis told her at the old hideout. Julia asked, "Is she alive?" and Francis replied, "I don't know. I can't tell. Just get an ambulance and tell the police where we are. And tell them to hurry!"

The police and paramedics showed up quickly. The girls finally showed up too, and the police told everyone to stand back. The paramedics checked the body and confirmed that she was dead, then radioed in to the hospital that they had a DOA. Stacie fainted and was taken to the hospital by another paramedic.

After the ambulance left and everyone was taken home by their parents, Tim thought, *Mandan was killed by Big Foot, but why are these creatures killing? What the hell did we ever do to them?* It was then that they all thought life here on the rez would never be the same.

Chapter Seven

To Believe

One afternoon a week after Mandan's funeral, there were two policemen putting up notices on the doors of everyone's home in town. It read: "To the people of Grey Stalk. There is an urgent meeting in the auditorium at the high school tonight at 6:00 p.m. Everyone must attend."

When the time came to go, everyone was showing up. The parking lot was getting full. All the kids sat together and wondered what the meeting was about. A man came out on the stage and said, "Welcome, all of you. I guess you are all wondering what this meeting is all about, so I'll get right down to business. First of all, my name is Elton. I teach first grade here at Grey Stalk. I was raised here. I'm sure a lot of you know me. And, like you, I'm wondering about all these killings and kidnappings. Where did these creatures come from, and why? Why are they doin' this to us?"

As he talked about each creature in detail, the people listened. For the first time, children listened to what was being said and were not playing around in their seats. Alter explaining what these creatures were, Elton said, "I now want to draw your attention to my great grandpa." He was 115 years old, but he looked like he was in his 70s. He said hi to everyone as he stood on stage at the podium.

He was not mad but spoke with a loud and stern voice. His voice was so loud the building shook as if God were speaking to these people himself. The old man said, "You young generation! You started all this. You started all this yourself. You brought these creatures to us. It is because of you and your lack of respect. It is because of your disbelief in stories told about these creatures. These stories were told long, long ago, before I was a child. They were told to our tribe because they were true then. And they were told not to frighten young children, or so they won't stay out after dark. I want you to believe in these stories for yourselves and others. I want you all to continue telling these stores about these creatures from long ago. This is how you'll put these creatures back where they came from. Back into stories, stories that made some of our people's legends.

"I know a lot of you lost friends, family, and relatives in the past several weeks. I am sorry of your loss. This is payment for bringing these creatures to life. I hope you all learn something from this. I hope from now on you will respect what your elders tell you, even if it's just a story. Because you'll learn something from it. Now go home and pray for your family, friends, and relatives that died or went missing this summer. And pray for yourself just as you pray for others who are living. And remember, never to stop believing in these stories. Only then will you put these creatures back into the stories they came from. Thank you," he said, and he walked off the stage. He was known as a medicine man. The white people called him a healer and a prophet.

As they were leaving the auditorium, Elton asked, "Great Grandpa, why are you smiling?" He answered, "I sense good feelings from our people now. And I think we'll have real stories once again." Elton just shook his head in a yes motion and said, "Yeah," with a smile.

As everyone was leaving the auditorium, they talked about what they had heard, and said they were going to do what the old man said. Everyone went home. Everyone prayed. The gang prayed just as the old man said to do. The next day was long but peaceful. The evening came, and nothing happened because everyone believed nothing would happen. Everyone felt peace had returned to Grey Stalk and the creatures had returned back to the stories told long ago and of today. Big Foot, Goat Man, the little men, and Olga and her wolf all disappeared from reality.

It was a Saturday morning, and Francis woke up and got out of bed. He felt tired. He felt like he had been up for a couple of days with little sleep. He asked his mom why he felt that way, and she said, "We all do, honey, because we used our bodily energy and our minds with prayer to do what the old man told us to do." Francis said, "Oh."

Francis called Julia and said, "Hey, girl, are you ready for school?" She answered, "No!" Francis asked, "How are you feeling?" She replied, "A little tired, but OK." Francis told her, "Well, I'll see you in school. See ya." She said, "I love you," because he could not hear her. He was already off the phone. He went out on his porch and stretched, saying to himself, "Me and some of my friends got hurt, and two of my other friends died. I wonder how next summer's gonna be?"

The End

About the Author

Eric Bell is a full blooded Apache and half Chiricahua from Mescalero, New Mexico. He is also half San Carlos from Arizona. Born in Phoenix Arizona, but raised on the Mescalero Apache Indian Reservation in New Mexico. He wants to pursue his writing to share stories for people of all ages to enjoy.

CPSIA information can be obtained
at www.ICGtesting.com
Printed in the USA
FFHW020813191218
49919295-54542FF